Praise fo

"Iain Ryan's *Four Day*
police procedural. Far
and James Ellroy will find much to admire here; Ryan is the punked-up disciple of these geniuses, and he's stripped this baby down so it's all muscle, all meanness, a brutal ride through corrupt Brisbane in the '80s. Read this, and thank me when it's on your best-of-the-year list. A hell of a debut."

—William Boyle, author of *Gravesend* and *Death Don't Have No Mercy*

"A streamlined epic of sex, violence and corruption told with lean, elegant prose and featuring a harrowing climax that will blister your eyeballs. Iain Ryan ducks your defenses and gets in close to deliver literary rabbit punches to the kidneys that'll leave you bleedy and eager for more punishment."

—Jedidiah Ayres, author of *Peckerwood* and *Fierce Bitches*

"Pure in its darkness, and perfect in its terror, *Four Days* is a brilliant debut."

—David Whish-Wilson, author of *Zero at the Bone* and *Line of Sight*

"Iain Ryan has learned the lessons of the modern maestros James Ellroy, Ken Bruen, and James Sallis, but his poetry and cadence is completely Australian."

—Peter Doyle, author of *The Big Whatever* and *Crooks Like Us*

A Broken River Books original
10765 SW Murdock LN
Apt. G6
Tigard, OR 97224

Although some of the broader historical events described in this book are drawn from the documented history of Brisbane, the events and characters in this book (including, for the avoidance of doubt, the police officers and their actions) are completely fictional and imaginary; any resemblance they might bear to actual circumstances or to a living person is entirely coincidental.

ISBN: 978-0-9943121-0-5

Cover design by Iain Ryan and Carl Chipperfield.
Interior design by Iain Ryan and J David Osborne
Editing by J David Osborne and Gabriella West.

www.iainryan.com

Printed in the USA.

IAIN RYAN

FOUR DAYS

BROKEN RIVER BOOKS
PORTLAND, OR

For Lee Earle

PROLOGUE
TUNNEL ISLAND
2003

JIM HARRIS WALKED THE dark path. The scrub was thick around the headland — high dry grass and short trees — but it couldn't slow the coming storm. The southerly wind blasted in over the ocean, washing Harris back and forth as he stumbled along. It was a bad night for it but he knew the way. He diverted off into the raw bush land and arrived at a set of timber stairs. At the top, up above the canopy, he came to a wall. There was a gate, a box mounted beside it. He opened the box and pressed the intercom.

"It's me," he shouted, over the gale.

The gate buzzed open.

Harris made his way up The Theodor Club's long lawn, past the pool and rock garden, to the rear entry. A security guard stood by the door. As Harris approached, he nodded into his earpiece and stepped away. Inside, The Theodor was busy for a Tuesday. Most of the booths were full. Stray businessmen sat by the bar. A couple slow danced in the corner. Behind them, the club's banner — a tall, red curtain — ran floor to ceiling. At the far end of the curtain, a girl let him through.

"Same room as always," she said. "But Jackie called in sick. You've got the new girl. I tried to call."

He stopped.

"She knows her stuff," said the girl.

"Okay."

He found the room and knocked.

A tall brunette opened up. She had crisp green eyes and wore a white terrycloth robe, a gold chain resting on her chest. The resemblance was immediate and uncanny, almost painful.

"Damn, you're right on time," she said. "Come in. I'm Lauren."

She had everything laid out. He went to the bed and looked at the uniform.

"Policeman, huh?" she said.

He shrugged and started to unbutton his shirt.

"You want a drink?"

He shook his head. He couldn't let his eyes rest on hers. "I don't drink," he said.

"Right. I might actually have a little bump, if that's okay? It helps me work."

"Sure."

"You want a go?"

He put the blue shirt on. "I'm even worse on the gear."

She laid out her drugs and snorted them back. With the uniform on, he went to the table and sat across from her. The coke pinned her eyes. They blazed. The hair was everywhere and it was long.

Memories volleyed for attention inside him.

The eyes. He could feel her in them.

She laughed a little. "So, what's the story?"

"I want you to hurt me," he said.

PART ONE
CAIRNS
1984

FRIDAY, SEPTEMBER 14, 1984

HE FUCKED UP AND they sent him back to Cairns. Back to the beginning. Back to Sarah Hannon. And back to this. She stood by the window and smoked, the shirt of her police uniform hanging open.

He said, "You ever think about leaving?"

She pointed the cigarette out the window and said, "What? And miss all this?"

Harris went to her. He took the smoke from her hand and sucked out a long drag. Down below, the city stretched out to the sea. It looked the same, exactly the same.

"Brisbane didn't do much for you," she said.

"It got me out of uniform."

"And yet here we are," she said.

"Here we are."

Ten years later.

He'd loved her since high school. She was married now. The higher-ups in the Brisbane Police Department knew the score. They had just the right penance in mind. They sent him home.

* * *

The whole thing was a case of bad luck. In Brisbane, no one crossed the Agrioli family. They were a protected species and Harris knew it. But the Agriolis had a new recruit, a cousin fresh out of the clink, and Harris didn't know him. He should have known. The fat prick looked just like the rest of them.

If only he'd had his head together.

It didn't turn out that way.

The new Agrioli guy, Roberto, decided to lay a hand to one of the working girls. They were all in The Roxy and Harris caught a glimpse of it. He knew the girl, some kid from Dalby, barely out of her teens. Harris didn't see how it started but it ended with Roberto screaming in her face. He had her backed over a pool table, his huge hand wrapped around her throat. It was a bad scene. Tears poured out of the girl while all the dumb fucks watched on, drinks in hand.

Harris moved fast. His first blow caught Roberto in the side, opening him up. He took a handful of the man's scalp and hit him hard in the center. That's all it took. Roberto went over, splitting his head open on the way down. The last clear thing Harris remembered was the spray of blood hitting his shirt. Then something heavy slammed in from behind.

He came to in a squad car.

"Where are we?"

The beat cop in the passenger seat didn't even turn around.

"This dickhead has nine lives," he said.

The driver laughed. "Eight now."

Harris woke up in hospital.

"You fucked up, Jim," said the Inspector. He sat by the bed. "You fucked up bad. Worse than you think. A lot worse."

That's why they sent him north.

Sarah Hannon put her hand up to the window. Rain thrashed the glass. The long monsoon of September '84. He unzipped her skirt and let it fall. She went to the bed and took the rest off.

"Close the blinds."

The dark made it worse. Her body felt the same. Full breasts and thighs. She breathed hard, her hand on the same part of his shoulder as always. The history and chaos sliding back into him.

They hadn't lasted a week before ending up here. It scared him. Harris knew her. She was, and probably always would be, a hole he couldn't crawl out of.

Couldn't and wouldn't.

He had to say it out loud: "We were kidding ourselves about this never happening again."

She didn't answer. She kept moving under him.

He closed his eyes.

"We should stop," he said. "This is crazy."

"We're not stopping."

Three hours later Sarah was back with her husband and Harris knelt on the tiles, wiping vomit from his face.

It went on for months.

TUESDAY, OCTOBER 9, 1985

BUILT TO WITHSTAND BLAZING sun and humidity, the Cairns police station had a dank, muted feel to it in the rain. There was never enough light. Every desk had a lamp. They were all on today, except his.

"You okay?"

Harris wiped his eyes. A young constable stood in the doorway. His name was Pete or Rob or Sam, something like that. He was the only copper in Cairns who gave Harris the time of day. He was in the sin bin as well.

"Bulb's blown?" said Harris.

"I'll have a look around. You don't look so good, sir. You want to go back to the hotel?"

"No, I'll just have a…" Harris opened a drawer and scratched around for his box of aspirin. "Do they need us?"

"McArthur wants us for an arson up the coast."

"What is it?"

"Nothing serious. Fire on church property. No casualties."

"And they need a CIB detective for this? No prizes for guessing the denomination, then."

"I guess not, sir."

"You go to church?" said Harris. He dropped the painkillers into a dry glass.

"Only on Sunday," said the constable. "It's Sam, sir. Sam Peters."

"Peters, right. Go get the car."

The job was a wash. An hour's drive and a straight-up public ass-kissing at the other end. A priest had been storing the parish hand-me-downs in a shipping container out on the road. In the night, someone set the thing on fire. Case closed. After a cup of tea with the minister and the old lady who called it in, they all went and stood under umbrellas and peered into the container. One of the doors hung open and Peters yanked the other back. The smell of charcoal, burnt plastic, and hair drifted out.

"I don't know why anyone would do this," said the priest.

"It's bloody kids," said Harris.

Peters turned his flashlight on. They stood at the mouth of the thing and watched the beam scan around. Harris's stomach churned at the thought of a body or a torso propped up in the ash. The thing was empty.

"Write it up," he said.

"What now?" said the old lady.

"In this rain, there's not much we can do."

The priest lit a cigarette. He was an old bloke, on his last go-round. "I went to bed last night and I just knew I should have padlocked it. I just knew it." He took another drag and the smoke hung under the umbrella like a cloud. "So, no chance of finding these kids, then, I guess?"

Harris looked at Peters.

"We'll look around," he said. "But I don't think we'll find them. You probably have a better idea than us."

The priest nodded. "The things the Lord reveals belong to us, the rest we have to accept, I guess."

"It's all the Lord's work," said the old lady.

Harris stared back into the container.

"This will teach you two for doing the right thing."

In the car, Peters turned the engine over and put the wipers to full. "I know a place for lunch," he said. "You need to get back, sir?"

Harris shook his head.

"And enough with this *sir* shit."

They drove out to the highway and north to Port Douglas. Peters had a relative working the bar at the Court House Hotel and for two hours they sat upstairs and drank and watched the gray sky drizzle down into the ocean.

The beer helped. Harris started to come back to himself. Peters could hold his drink.

Harris asked him, "You married?"

"Not yet. There's no one up here. You?"

"Nah, not cut out for it."

"I figure Brisbane is where I want to be."

"There's a lot of people there, mate," said Harris. "It was a shock to me when I first moved down, let me tell you."

"Yeah, I figure it's the spot," said Peters.

Harris slept most of the way home, and it was dark when they got in. There was a note waiting at the station desk: some of the Brisbane licensing boys were flying in. They requested his presence at the hotel bar, five-thirty, night after next. Harris tossed the note and started back to the hotel on foot. He was a block away when Peters pulled up beside him in a battered white utility.

"Get in."

As they pulled up at the hotel, Peters glanced past him. Harris turned. Sarah Hannon, in plain clothes, front and center in the lobby, clear as day.

Harris turned back. "You know Constable Hannon?"

"We went through the academy together."

"She's an old friend."

"Okay," said Peters, but Harris caught it. The kid had slept with her or knew her well enough. One of the two, and either was too much when it came to Sarah. As Harris waved Peters off, the kid looked more worried than jealous. That wasn't a good sign.

Hannon showered.

Harris poured himself another drink.

Cairns lay dead in its grave. Eight o'clock, barely a car on the road. Lights off.

The phone rang. He let it go.

Hannon came back out, dressed to the nines. "I've got to go. I'm supposed to be out with the girls."

"How bright's this bloke of yours?"

"He's a PE teacher, Jim." She ran a hand down the side of his face, the tips of her fingers brushing through his beard. "I should never have married him. You know that, right?"

"You should never have married anyone."

Her green eyes burned.

She slapped him and walked.

The silent TV sprayed light over the room. He found himself sitting up in the bed. Must have been asleep.

The phone was ringing again.

He rolled over and picked it up.

"Harris," he said.

"I heard you slithered back into town. If you had any brains at all in that thick fucking head of yours, you'd go back to Brisbane where you belong."

"Dad?"

The line went dead.

WEDNESDAY, OCTOBER 10, 1985

HARRIS STARED INTO THE bathroom mirror and cursed his luck. Fuck Hannon. Fuck this dawn of the dead Cairns bullshit and its furnace heat creeping in at four in the morning. And fuck Agrioli, the fat fuck. Harris moved closer to his reflection. The city had already taken its toll. The skin under his eyes hung dark and loose. A sheen of sweat covered his bulk. His broad shoulders had started to slacken. A paunch protruded from his wife-beater. He pushed a hand over the gravelly skin of his face and tugged at his cheeks. He closed his eyes.

Fuck Jim Harris.

It wasn't all about luck.

That night in the nightclub in Brisbane had started the same way as a hundred others. Knock-off drinks with the boys, dinner-drinks with Dyer, his partner — a much younger man — and then late-night drinks in some club in the valley.

It wasn't any old club that night. It was The Roxy. Shit-hole to end all shit-holes. The Agriolis had it stitched up. People could buy just about anything in there.

Harris kept to the bar. He stayed in the dark, smoked his cigarettes, and let Dyer work the room. The kid brought girls back. One of them spoke like an American, smelled of weed and soap. He must've been drunk because they all ended up in a booth together, four drunk girls and two drunk cops. Harris usually wouldn't let it happen.

Dyer hit the dance floor. Three of the girls followed.

The American stayed behind. She turned the ends of her hair in her fingers and said:

"So, you're a cop?"

Harris nodded. He scanned the room.

"You must see all kinds of things?"

"That's right."

"Great club."

Harris nudged the cherry off his cigarette.

"You don't say much," she said.

There was even less for him in that than the other questions. She shimmied round closer.

"I like older men. You all have a story."

"I don't have a story."

"I'm sure you do."

"Not me. I forget my stories. What about you? What's your story?"

"I'm a writer."

Harris looked at her.

"Yeah, what do you write?"

"Short stories, mainly."

"Any good?"

"They sell. I can do it anywhere."

The tells said otherwise. Harris's cop brain twitched. Hooker. Drug dealer. Student. Checkout girl. Cleaner. He looked at her a little harder. No, trust fund. Slumming it. The jewelry and make-up too understated for this far down the food chain. A tourist.

"And you spend your downtime fucking old men?" said Harris. "Sounds like quite a life."

"Don't be like that."

"I'm just…" He shook his head.

She waited a beat. "You from here?"

"You should go home. And you should stay there," he said.

"Oh, boy."

"No, that's right. This isn't the place for you."

"But I'm with a policeman," she said. The last part in a high, sing-song voice. She came closer.

Harris felt the warmth of her hand seep through his trousers. He left it there, in spite of himself. He froze. She looked good. Her eyes caught the strobe light.

"Come on, Mr. Policeman, what does a sister have to do?"

"What?" he said. He recoiled. Fucking Americans and their slang. Harris could see it now.

"What? What's wrong, big man?" she said. "Do you want to arrest me? Is that it? Come here. You can arrest me. You can do whatever you like."

"No. What did you say?"

The hand disappeared.

She saw him then.

What is wrong with you?" she said.

"There's nothing wrong with me."

"Jesus. Yeah, I don't know about that."

The girl grabbed her purse off the table and started rummaging through it.

Harris squeezed out of the booth and walked. He used the bathroom. He stood beside some punk in the bathroom mirror. The punk glanced quickly at his reflection, nervous. Harris stared him down. The punk bolted. He turned back to the mirror.

"Lachlan," he said, quietly.

On his way back to the bar he came past the pool tables. That's where he saw Roberto Agrioli hit the girl. That was the time and the place and the moment. That was the exact start of the trouble.

THURSDAY, OCTOBER 11, 1985

THE BRISBANE LICENSING BOYS were notorious grafters and thugs, but they were also a complicated lot. They weren't corrupt to a man. In Brisbane CIB, enough of them — a small percentage — were clean enough, and this made the whole squad formidable. No one knew exactly who was in on The Joke, as they called it. So with licensing, Harris chose to roll with the punches. They had a lot of clout and for whatever reason — none of them good — they looked after him.

They were all operating under the auspices of Detective Sergeant Barry Caller. Caller was one of the true power brokers on the force. He scared people. Always a man with a lot of friends and no enemies. Harris met him years back on a routine suicide, some old timer who lived above The Prince Hotel. Caller knew the bloke. He came down to the scene and had a sniff around. Afterwards, he shouted Harris a drink and got down to it: "Jim, this dickhead had a few good reasons to check out. Pull his file if you like, but I'd personally appreciate it if you didn't waste a lot of police resources on this shit. Just let this one sit."

Harris waved his glass at the barmaid. "It didn't look like anyone else pulled the trigger in there."

It was true. The old man was locked in. He had his hands around the rifle in a way no one could stage. It was no whodunnit.

"That's the spirit," said Caller.

"Serve and protect," said Harris.

The following day, Harris pulled the file anyway. Victim was Carlos Harding, seventy-four, priors for soliciting and assault. A short stint in Boggo Road for B&E. A real model citizen.

Harris closed it off.

Caller turned up at the station urinal not long after. "You never know when you'll need a good man in homicide," he said under his breath.

Harris laughed. "I'll let you know when I run into one."

That was that. He was in.

Barry Caller now sat with his back to the restaurant wall in Cairns. The man had gone to seed in recent years, had the jowls of a retiree, a round gut resting against the table. He hunched over the menu like a toad, shaking his head. "Love, I think I'll have the beef and black bean with fried rice." He turned the menu over, held it up. "Do you have tallies? Where are the fucking tallies?"

The waitress smiled. She had no idea what he was on about.

"A tallie," said Blintiff. "The bigger bottle."

Ray Blintiff was the group's enforcer, rumored to be Caller's second in command. He towered over the table. Neat as a pin: clean-shaven, dark hair slicked down in a rigid part. His scalp had an icy whiteness to it.

"Fuck it," said Caller. "Just bring me another Fourex," and he shook the beer bottle at her. "Who picked this dump? Was it you, Jangles?"

Bobby Hearst. The Greek. They called him Jangles because he had the slightest bit of Mediterranean tint to him.

Jangles shrugged.

The rest of them kept ordering, shouting fast across the table.

"No, that's right. This is your fucking fault," said Caller, pointing at the new kid, some constable. They introduced him as David Thompson. Harris didn't know him. He was young, green. He didn't look familiar: baby-faced, couldn't have been much past twenty-two. Yet he was tired in the eyes. Bone tired. And uncomfortable in his civvies, too. Not long out of uniform. Harris remembered it well. There was an itch to it when the blues came off.

Thompson played it demure. "Last time I was in here, boss, they had them. I swear." He turned to the waitress and made a show with his hands. "The big bottle. Large bottle, large."

She finally got it. "Yes, yes, lar, lar." She turned and screamed something in Chinese back to the kitchen. A kitchen hand stepped out with a tallie of Fourex Bitter, holding it up like a trophy.

The table cheered.

"Thank fucking Christ for that," said Blintiff.

"Another win for the golden boy," said Caller.

Thompson took a long, shaky pull on his drink.

Harris looked around. He was starting to feel a lot like the new kid himself. "So are you fellas up here on business?"

Blintiff shut it down. "After dinner, mate."

They ate and Jangles paid with a roll of cash. On the sidewalk, the crew stood around and smoked. Half of them still had beers in hand. They didn't even think twice. It gave Harris a bad feeling. Caller took him a little further up the street and handed him a smoke.

"We've got to go and see some people tonight, Jim, and we've got a bit of a problem. You know Marty Kendal?"

Harris knew him.

The smoke had a sweet taste to it.

"Am I smoking what I think I'm smoking?" said Harris.

"Just to help you relax," said Caller. "Fucking Marty had the day off yesterday. And he decided to have himself a little party out at the dogs. He's supposed to be here with us, but the stupid prick ended up in hospital with alcohol poisoning. Can barely stand up. Can't fly. Good to no one. Now we've got to go and see these people who've been misbehaving, and we could use an extra set of hands."

"You need anything in particular?"

"Just your discretion, Detective Harris, that's all. Just your discretion."

They took two cars: a squad car from the station and a grey land cruiser they'd hired at the airport. Harris rode with Caller and Blintiff in the cruiser. They had him in the back. "You bring your sidearm, Harris?" said Blintiff, eyes locked to his in the rearview.

"Hand it over," said Caller.

Harris did it.

Caller opened the glove box and took out a white cloth bag and put the gun inside. He unholstered his own pistol and put it in alongside. "Don't let me forget this is in here," he said.

Harris started to sweat, even with the windows wound. The rain had moved south. Now the humidity was back like the plague. Cairns was reeling. It was Friday night and the outskirts were quiet. A few drunks staggering home. A group of the local blacks milled about. No real trouble brewing. With the squad car rolling past in front, everyone kept their eyes averted.

Jangles pulled the car over about fifteen minutes out of town, out on the fringe, where the houses started to taper off into scrub. Blintiff pulled in alongside. He left the engine running and got out.

The Thompson kid said, "Richardson Street is next on the left and the Relaxo is at the end of the cul-de-sac. Number seventeen, the two-story place with a red mailbox out front. That's how the punters spot it."

"Okay," said Caller. "Thompson, Jangles, you're going in through the front. Harris, you're with us out back."

Blintiff opened the cruiser's rear cabin and dragged a sports bag out onto the asphalt. He took a shotgun out and handed it to Jangles. He handed the kid a revolver, gave another to Caller, and pushed one towards Jim. "Take it," he said. He pumped and loaded a sawn-off rifle for himself.

Caller pointed at each of them, "You listen to me. We go in, we get them all into the lounge room and put them on the ground. We'll have a little chat to the boys, then we're out of there. You got it? We're not shooting anyone. We're not arresting anyone. We're in and out, five or ten minutes. You all got it?"

The all murmured their agreement.

Harris checked the gun.

The house was a wreck. Creeping in around the side wasn't much of an option. Blintiff took one step into the brittle frangipani leaves carpeting the yard and gave up on subtlety, running the rest. The others followed suite, taking the place the hard way. Blintiff and Harris made it to the top of the rear stairs just as Jangles kicked in the front door.

A naked man came out first. Blintiff caught him in the stomach with his free hand and kept moving.

"I got this dickhead," said Caller behind them.

Inside, a series of half-naked women streamed out of a hallway into the kitchen.

"Get into the fucking living room," screamed Blintiff, pushing them through an alcove, barely seeing them.

Harris provided cover as they took the hallway. Blintiff kicked in the first door and dragged a bloke out by the hair. As he worked on the guy, a porcelain mug sailed out, missing his head by an inch. Blintiff dropped the man and stepped back in. He reappeared with a woman, a fistful of her hair wrapped around his hand.

Further down, a shot sounded and someone started screaming, a man.

Harris moved, stepping around Blintiff. A tall, broad man came out of a doorway, covered in blood. Harris brought his gun up. The man raised his hands. Harris went to him and whipped him across the face, the force slamming the man's torso into the wall. When he was down, Blintiff grabbed him by the ankle and yanked him along the boards for another beating.

Harris kept moving. He went to the end of the corridor and found Jangles in a bedroom. He stood by the end of a bed, holding himself up. A gun lay at his feet. "I'm fine," jangles yelled. "Sorry. Shit."

"You hit?"

"That cunt just tried to shoot me. You get him?"

"He's down," said Harris.

Jangles wiped his face. "Jesus."

"Are you hit, mate?"

"Nah, I don't think so." Jangles checked himself. "That's his blood, I think."

Across the hall, Harris could hear Thompson raising hell in the other room. Four women sprinted out and Blintiff went in after them. Harris followed. Another man, fully dressed, stood propped up against the wall by the door. He'd been belted a few times but his eyes were open. Blintiff grabbed him. "Go get Thompson," he said. "Check the porch. This should be the last of them."

Harris walked the long room alone. The place was curtained-off, like a makeshift hospital ward. No line of sight and no cover. He stayed low, flipped open each section, gun at waist level. "If any of you ladies are still in here, it's time to leave," Harris shouted. He crept further in. He checked another of the chambers, then another. Something moved down the end.

Harris crept up, ripped the curtain back. A girl, ten or twelve, stood in the corner of the partition holding a cat. She had her eyes squeezed shut, her nightie wet with urine. They had the partition dollied up like a kid's bedroom. Her drawings were on the wall.

"Come on, sweetie. It's okay," he said. "Bring the cat."

Harris hoisted her up and carried her and the cat back to the kitchen. As they passed the living room he noted the carnage. The boys had everyone, man and woman, lying face down on the living room carpet. Caller was screaming at them, "...and you don't fucking do that without the permission of our good friends the Sienna family, and you..."

Harris took the girl out to the rear landing and sat her down in the corner. "Wait here, and don't move." He turned back to the house and stopped. David Thompson stepped out of the sleep-out, made his way through the kitchen and onto the terrace. He had a young woman behind him, holding his hand. She looked like a teenager. Thin and scared.

Harris stepped out of the dark corner just as they reached the stairs. "Hey, kid."

Thompson spun around, brought the gun up.

"It's me," said Harris.

The kid was wild-eyed. Tears lined his face.

They stared at each other.

Thompson shook his head. He kept the gun aimed and took the stairs backwards, one at a time. As Harris watched them run across the back yard, the little girl said, "I want to go with Laura."

The licensing boys filed out. Harris the scene in quickly as he passed through the lounge. Ten or so women laid out on the floor, stock still. All the men were borderline unconscious, lying face up. Two other women, slightly older, knelt in a corner. Someone had slapped them around a little. The little girl ran to one of them. No one said a word.

Harris was the last out. Blintiff stopped him, "Where's Thompson?"

"He took off with one of the girls."

"What?"

"I saw him run across the yard as I cleared the sleep-out."

Caller sent Jangles back to look for them.

They all waited out on the sidewalk.

Jangles reappeared. He shrugged.

"He could be back at the car," said Harris.

"We gotta go," said Blintiff.

They ran.

Harris rode with Jangles. As they tore up the road's shoulder, Jangles screamed, "What did this bird look like?" He was still half-deaf from the gunshot back in the house.

"Young. Attractive. White, five-one or so, brown hair."

Jangles nodded. He didn't drive back towards the station house. Instead, he steered the car across town and back out to the southern highway. Caller and Blintiff weren't following. Half an hour out of Cairns, Jangles pulled into a dirt road and headed for the beach.

"What's this?" said Harris.

"Settle down. Just a last bit of business for the night. I think you'll like it." He took a hip flask out of his jacket and took a nip. He handed it over. "This'll help," he said.

Harris drank.

The two of them stood in the deserted car park and waited. A half moon sat low in the sky overhead. The ocean rumbled. Harris watched the lights of a ship creep across the horizon. On their third cigarette, a van came down the track and swerved a little as it turned onto the asphalt. Music thumped. The side door opened and out of the bright interior stepped Barry Caller. Two women came out behind him. The rear door popped and Blintiff draped his legs out, fastening his trousers. Another two women followed. The driver, a squat Italian in footy shorts and a white V-neck tee, had a girl in tow also.

"Boys," said Caller. "Look what I found."

Jangles sucked hard on his cigarette, "Where's Thomo?"

"He's your partner, shit-for-brains," said Blintiff.

"Don't you worry about Constable Thompson," said Caller. "He can look after himself."

"But is he looking after himself?" said Jangles.

Caller put his arm around Jangles and walked him back to the van. They spoke for a moment. Jangles nodded as he lifted out a carton of beer.

On the beach, the women decided to go swimming. They ran down to the water's edge and stripped off, dragging Jangles with them. Caller opened the carton and handed out the drinks, "Harris, this is Sal. He's a mate of ours from up here. Sal, Jim grew up in Cairns."

"Did he now?" said Sal. "He don't look so familiar to me. Must have been a good boy when he lived up here."

"What *did* you do up here?" said Caller.

Harris cracked the beer and took a long swallow. "Nothing much. I wasn't a copper up here."

Blintiff drained his in two pours and tossed it. "Okay, fuck you poofs, I'm off," he said. He unbuttoned his shirt and walked down to the water in his briefs. He had a flashlight. He started waving it around.

"What's he up to?" said Harris.

Caller laughed, "He's hung like a fucking donkey. He always likes to show them before he slips it in."

The Italian built a fire and the party got underway. Caller disappeared further up the beach. Jangles slammed beers and prodded the fire. When he started necking one of the women, Harris made his way down to the waterline to smoke. After a time, the Italian came out after him. He had a young woman with him.

"This is Melinda," said the Italian. "She's a nice girl. You should try to enjoy yourself, Detective. I brought these girls especially to meet you. This one, Melinda, this one comes from Cairns."

"Does he now?" she said. "Detective, huh?"

The Italian came and stood beside him. He puffed on a cigar and they both stared out at the water. The girl moved down in front of Harris and opened his fly. She reached her hand in. The Italian patted him on the back, just as the girl started with her mouth. "That's more like it," he said.

Harris felt every drop of booze surge through him.

He stared at the ocean.

The Italian said, "You see that out there? That's the future, Detective. And this is how it feels, like a blow job from a young girl. You feel these things?"

"Fuck off," said Harris.

The Italian chuckled. "Okay," he said and moved away.

Harris looked down at the girl.

"What do you know about a place called the Palm Relaxo?" he said, feeling himself slur.

The girl dragged him down into the sand. "You don't wanna go there. That's what I know."

Harris woke at dawn. He was alone. The beach stretched out around him. He had sand in his hair. A warm six-pack of beer sat tucked in beside him. As soon as he sat up, the nausea hit him. He cracked a beer and pushed it down. He took another into the ocean. The water helped. As he dressed, he found a set of keys in his shoes. In the car park, a note sat under the front wiper of the squad car. It read: GLOVE BOX.

He got in behind the wheel and popped the box. Inside he found his service revolver and tied around the barrel was a used condom.

That was the end of the licensing boys.

FRIDAY, OCTOBER 12
TO
FRIDAY, FEBRUARY 2, 1985

CALLER WENT BACK TO Brisbane and pulled some strings. The higher-ups listened; they cut Harris's transfer short. He had another four months in Cairns instead of twenty. It still felt like years. The warm rain swept back in and the job became the usual grind, endless errands. Aside from a weekend brawl, a dumped car in the CBD and a man found dead in a caravan (food poisoning), the city was as still as bay water. He let Sam Peters attend to most of it.

After each shift, Harris sat alone in the hotel bar. Every couple of nights Sarah Hannon showed up. They drank together and made small talk before heading upstairs. Things got bad. Harris could feel it all slipping. He started calling her. Begging.

His last month, she stayed over more often. Her husband's father was on the way out so they could sit up in Harris's room and drink and fuck ad nauseam. As Harris peeled back the veneer of Hannon, she seemed worse than ever. She had a new set of pills with her, a hundred bad ideas, and a thousand hurtful things to say in-between.

Harris lapped it up. He lifted back the sheets of his bed and dragged her over to him, time and time and time again.

"Come inside me," she said.

He did it.

They went out on the final Sunday, a restaurant on the broad water. The rain kept coming. In the candlelight, Hannon stared in her compact and said:

"You going to talk to him before you go?"

"He's been calling me," said Harris.

She looked away, "He calls me sometimes. But not one for a chat, is he?"

"No. Sammy never was one for talking."

She winced at his name. "You think he'll ever get past it?"

"That's not who he is."

The waiter came. Hannon asked for another glass of wine. She took a prawn and snapped it open.

"So, back to Brisbane," she said. "I don't know what you did, but it worked."

"You don't *want* to know."

"So I figured. That's the problem with you, Jim."

"Is it now?"

"You always know when you're doing the wrong thing."

"And yet…"

She nodded. "That's right," she said. "Lucky me."

As the week wore on, Harris stayed as drunk as possible. The last Monday, the last Tuesday. Time stood still.

The call from Peters snapped him out of it.

It came late in the night: "Hannon's in the hospital. She tried to kill herself." She did it on the last Thursday. Sleeping tablets and vodka, apparently.

Peter and Harris went in to see her. They watched as she took small, shallow breaths, passed out in the hospital bed with the lights on.

"I spoke to her partner. They caught a bad accident yesterday," said Peters. "Couple of kids in a camper van wrapped around the side of a truck. She's going to have to do the whole fucking bit before they let her back out there. She'll be off for a month or so, best case."

Harris stared at her. He still had Jangles's hip flask. He took it out and had a sip.

Peters turned it down.

"I want you to take care of her for me," said Harris.

"I'll do my best."

"I know what she's like. Just try," said Harris. On the way out, he saw the flowers. White roses off to the side, unopened. He checked the card.

It read:

YOU DESERVED THIS.

YOU'LL BE WITH LACHLAN SOON.

Harris tore the card in half and put the pieces in his pocket. He took the bouquet and walked.

Peters didn't say a word.

The spare key to Harris's family home was still in the same place it always was. He let himself in and walked through the living room, down the hall to the master bedroom. He kicked the door open without breaking stride and dragged his father from the bed, pulling him onto the floor by his arm. Harris stood over him, took the man's bony throat in his hands, and pushed the barrel of his gun flush against his head.

"Sammy, if you ever contact her again, I'll come back here and fucking shoot you."

He pulled the trigger four times.

Click.

Click.

Click.

Click.

His father hollered like an animal each time, through each of the empty chambers. Five hours later, Harris was on the plane back to Brisbane.

PART TWO
BRISBANE
1985

MONDAY, FEBRUARY 4, 1985

DETECTIVE CONSTABLE MATT DYER was a smart kid playing a long, greasy game. He was partnered with Harris to make sure it stayed that way. In the briefing, the Inspector was clear, "Dyer's old man used to be one of us. You make sure Matty doesn't rock the boat or you'll be washing squad cars the rest of your career." Dyer wasn't much of a detective. He had no real heart for it. Competent, but nothing more. The partnership was babysitting duty. It was resume padding. If they did their stint without trouble — if Harris didn't let Dyer get too dirty or too clean — they'd both be promoted. Dyer to upper management, Harris to something easy. It was a good arrangement, headed in the right direction, right up until Harris took down Roberto Agrioli in the nightclub.

Dyer was there. He missed the fight. He was busy. But he did go ahead and drive his date home in the squad car afterwards, something that got noticed after the fact. Verdict: they'd both fucked up. And they both got punished for it.

Harris went to Cairns.

In the meantime, they parked Dyer with Andrew Richardson and a series of dull arson cases out in the northern suburbs. “Fucking Richo,” said Dyer quietly. “He’d have happily stretched that thing out till Christmas. He’s probably still working them.”

It was an hour before knock-off. They’d given up looking busy. They sat beneath the flickering fluorescent lighting of Brisbane CIB. Harris yawned. The office was empty. Every other copper was assigned to a manhunt out in Gatton. They were bedded down out there, soaking up the overtime budget. The only officers left were Richardson and two older blokes working something “urgent” for vice.

“Look, mate,” said Harris. “I got back as soon as I could.”

“Thank fuck for that.”

“We’re not entirely out of the bad books yet.”

Dyer lit a smoke and took a measure of the situation. “Nope, not yet,” he said. “Jeez, I could have done with some of that OT.” He was a tall, thin kid, a bit too much polish to him for a policeman. Carried a comb like some of the old timers. Women went for it.

“Was it worth it?” said Harris.

Dyer caught on, the girl from the club. He stared into space, trying to dredge up the memory. He sighed. “Nope. Nothing really came of it. And nothing’s worth a month of riding along with Richo. I swear, that guy’s farts are part of the upholstery. We paid a mean price for our indiscretions, Jim, I’ll tell you that much. A mean price.”

Harris agreed.

No more stepping out of line.

THURSDAY, FEBRUARY 7, 1985

HARRIS WOKE UP WET with sweat. Something moved in the window, a hand rapping on the frosted louvers.

"Jim? Come on, mate."

He placed the voice: Dyer Senior. Roy. He gave up knocking. The old bloke was already halfway back to the house when Harris opened the door. It was still dark out, but dawn wasn't far off.

"What's going on?"

The old man didn't move too fast these days, especially in summer. He always wore the same uniform, a white short-sleeve shirt tucked into grey trousers. The eternal plainclothesman.

"They're calling you in early," Roy said. "Matty's in the shower."

Harris checked his watch: five fifteen.

"Bloody hell," said Harris. "What time do you get up?"

"Early. I've already got the billy on."

Harris went back inside. The flat looked like a student dive. He'd been in there for a year before the Cairns thing and it never looked any better. Plates of half-eaten food sat on the table. Clothes mounded in piles. He had to clear the beer cans from the sink — all dutifully poured out before bed — just to take a glass of water.

Up in the house, Matt Dyer sat beside his father at the table. They had breakfast laid out. It made Harris's stomach ache.

"Jesus. Bit of a rough landing, mate?" said Dyer Junior. "Put some trousers on. They've called us in."

"So I hear. What is it?"

"A body out in the suburbs. Coopers Plains." He was excited, eating fast.

"Okay," said Harris. "Shower first, I'll eat on the way. Give me five minutes."

By six they were in the car. Roy watched them go, standing under the awning light. Roy had a thing about backing out of the drive. As he waited, he patted his thigh, trying to call the neighbor's cat. The cat wasn't having it. There was something about him, something off.

"Is he okay?" said Harris.

"Dad? Yeah, he's fine."

Dyer took a quick look over at his father, honked the horn, and drove.

The body lay in a stretch of bush land, on a park reserve between residential houses and a suburban army barracks. Dyer took them off the highway, down into the streets. The sun was out. It was already warm enough to have the windows down. Harris watched the dirty weatherboard houses pan past. The knee-high grass, the panel-beaten cars, a hundred open windows. They came to the reserve entrance — an opening in a regular cul-de-sac — and stopped by a squad car sat parked across the road in front. A cadet waved them in.

The park wasn't much, a loping plane of treeless gravel. An asphalt track wound through it, ending just beside a small brick council building. Behind the building, the gravel and dirt tapered up into a long man-made hill, almost resembling a wall. They parked. Dyer grabbed the kit from the trunk and they walked up onto the wall. It was road-width at the summit, tapering off steeply on the other side.

"What the hell is this thing?" said Dyer.

"Beats me," said Harris. "Could be a flood levee."

They travelled along the earth wall until Harris spotted a small creek down along the plane on the far side. In the distance, past the creek, sat a tall patch of bush land. Light glowed inside it, trees and shrubs lit up like a campsite. Another squad car was parked down by the creek crossing. As they approached, he noticed a group of officers milling around.

Harris looked for familiar faces:

Fresh cadets.

Bored old-timers.

And Jillian McMurty, back in uniform, having been busted down from Vice the year previous. She saw him and waved her flashlight. "You guys walk here from CIB?" she said.

"Tell me you were first on," said Harris.

McMurty nodded. “Teenagers found her.” She pointed the flashlight at the squad car, two silhouettes in the back seat.

“Anything there?” said Dyer. He opened his notepad, marked the time.

“Hard to say,” said McMurty. “They’re pretty bombed. The girl thinks she may have seen your guy but…”

Harris turned to Dyer. “Leave the bag. Go and talk to them, then send them up to the station.”

Harris lit a cigarette. He draped it out of the corner of his mouth and squatted down to load the camera.

“Who’s in there?” he said, as he worked.

“The science blokes. The medical officer is due any minute.”

“How bad is it?”

He looked up at her and she shrugged her shoulders.

“Any ID?”

McMurty shook her head.

“What is it?” said Harris.

“There’s not much there, Jim.”

“Jesus.”

Dyer came back. “Okay, so—”

“Hang on,” said Harris.

They all turned and watched as the cadets tried to take the squad car back up the steep face of the earth wall. Dirt sprayed loose under the tires as they got about halfway up, swishing the car back and forth. The cadets got out. McMurty sent two other officers over to push. The kids in the back must have been freaking out.

"Why didn't we drive down here?" said Dyer with a smirk.

McMurty shook her head. "Those new guys are okay. I'd appreciate it if you didn't put this in your report. Our fearless leader back at the station house has a bug up his ass about the cars."

Dyer made another note.

"What did the kids say?" said Harris.

"Not much. The girl thought she caught a glimpse of someone, but they both need a coffee and a lie-down. So we going in?"

Harris stood there a moment. He looked the bush land over, searched the creek and the reserve and the earth wall. When he was ready, he said, "Lead the way, Jill."

A thin track snaked through the scrub and the body lay in a clearing not far in. It was off the track, hidden behind a thick bank of green lantana. McMurty took them in through a hole cut fresh in the scrub.

"Your guy probably came through a trench round further," she said. "And that's how I got in too, I'm afraid. It was dark when I got here."

"Anything left?" said Harris.

"Not in the trench, but there's boot prints around."

Inside the brush wall, the ground was carpeted with leaves and pine needles. In the center were the remains of a small fire and beside it lay the body of a dead girl.

The officers at the scene stopped working when they saw them. They backed up, gave the detectives space, five men with their flashlights pointed at the ground. Harris hated this part of it. The eerie silence that crept over a scene in this moment, it was always a bad omen. A sign of the impending weight. The other officers came and went, did their jobs, took their samples, and that was that. Harris had to live with it.

The first thing he noticed was the girl was small. The sun had not yet crept over the lantana, and Harris had to use his flashlight. She was white, late teens to early twenties, thin across the shoulders and hips. She had brown hair and it flayed out behind what was left of her skull. Her face was completely missing, a crater of blood and gore.

Harris pushed himself to keep looking, scanning down to the rest of her. She was naked except for a pair of stained white sport socks. She'd walked in them: mud and dirt was caked to her calves. The rest was troubling in a more subtle way. Her body, as always, had a cold stillness to it, made all the worse by the strange circular clearing she lay in.

Harris squatted down and looked the scene over. The science men had a few pieces marked off.

"So, what's the damage?" he said.

The science men glanced at each other. The government medical officer stepped around. "She hasn't been dead long. At a guess, a good one, I'd say she died late last night or very early this morning. Blunt instrument trauma to the face, neck, and shoulders. From the positioning and a cursory look, I'd say she's been sexually assaulted at some point."

"At some point?" said Dyer.

"Who are you?" said the officer.

"He's with me," said Harris.

The medical officer cleared his throat, "The injuries don't speak well of a…civil mind. I can't say in what order things happened. She has ligature marks around her wrists. Those marks on her arms and feet are consistent with drug use."

"But?" said Harris, hearing hesitation.

"I'm not sure of who did what. I suspect she was in very poor health leading up to her death. I couldn't say, right at this moment, what she was up to before she died."

Harris stood up and pointed to one of the science men he'd worked with before. "What have you got?"

"Not as much as we'd like."

They led them through it.

Clear boot prints, size eleven, more consistent with a laborer than a hiker.

Skin fragments under her nails.

Remnants of clothing in the fire.

Blood splatter indicating it all happened in the same place.

Divots in the ground around the body that could indicate the weapon.

No purse. No rings or jewelry. No ID.

Nothing.

Harris took photographs.

Dyer scratched away in his book. "I'll radio out for anyone at a loose end," he said.

Harris turned to McMurty. "We're short on the ground. If you know anyone off duty who'd come down, let them know. We'll need to grid search this scrub and go door to door anywhere within shouting distance. Okay you all, back to it, gents."

Three hours later they took the girl's body out and drove it away. As the day wore on, the investigation drew a crowd. The TV people came. The sun started to bake overhead. Harris spread a map and aerial photos over the hood of a car and looked at the size of it. The bush land was two miles across, not more than a short walk from everyday suburbia. Yet, from above, it was a dot hidden away in the houses, a real pocket of nowhere slipped into the gaps of the city.

THURSDAY, FEBRUARY 7, 1985

HARRIS AND DYER SPENT most of the day helping with the search, praying it would turn up a wallet or purse. Instead all they found was a rusted crowbar, a child's bike, and illegally dumped garbage, none of it relevant. The canvas of nearby houses turned up even less. No one heard her. No one saw her. No one saw any suspicious vehicles or a man returning to one on foot.

"We're fucked on this, aren't we?" said Dyer on the drive back to the office.

"Pretty much," said Harris.

They stopped at a burger place. Three forty PM.

Dyer had his notepad out. He ran it down. "We can do the autopsy at seven, get a run-down from Richo and the Vice boys before they clock off in… two hours. What do you want to do?"

"Call the police," said Harris.

"I wish. We're gonna be lumped with this. I bet you they just keep us with Richo and the other retirees for this."

"That Gatton thing is a fucking mess, mate. You've got dead kids. Their godfather has some clout with the Nats, apparently. No one's coming in this week. We're it. I might be able to persuade one or two of the licensing boys to check the brothels over, if they're feeling generous."

"There's no chance she's a citizen, right?" said Dyer.

"None. You see those marks on her?"

"I saw them," he said. "One doesn't automatically mean the other these days."

"It does in this game."

"She could come from money," said Dyer.

"Oh yeah, she could be a fucking poet or a ballerina, for all we know," said Harris. "Finish that. I need to take a proper break."

They left the car by the burger place and walked to a grimy pub across the street. Dyer kept to water and worked the case, occasionally making calls on the bar phone and checking the car radio. Harris sat by the window and drank himself steady.

They interviewed the teenagers from the bush land separately. Dyer took the girl, Harris the boy. He was a burly-looking kid for his age, hair long at the back and short at the sides, a cut that made no sense to Harris. The boy wore a flannel shirt and jeans and looked like he'd been living it up for a while.

"How you feeling?" said Harris, sliding a cup of tea and a smoke across the table.

"I don't smoke," said the kid.

"Don't smoke?"

"Asthma."

"So what happened?"

The boy told the story. They were bedded down together — him and the girl — until she saw a man run past over his shoulder. They scouted around, wondering where the guy sprung from.

"She could smell the fire. We know that clearing. We've been in there before," he said. "We could've ended up there. I don't even remember why we didn't."

"Because you got lucky. You two were high, right?" said Harris. "Tell the truth, fuckhead. No one's getting into trouble."

"We shared a joint on the way over."

"What about the asthma?"

He shrugged.

Dyer's girl could at least give them a description: probably white, probably male, probably thirty-plus, or older, short dark hair. In a jumpsuit of some sort, a tracksuit maybe. He didn't look at her, or not that she remembered. All he did was run past.

"How did these kids not hear her?" said Harris.

Dyer tapped a ruler on the side of the desk.

"Stoned, I guess."

"What time did they have?"

Dyer looked it up in the file. "She maintains they got there around midnight. Our girl could have been dead by then. There might not have been much to hear."

"If there was any?"

"What do you mean?"

"It's not always like that, mate."

They watched the autopsy. Dyer still didn't have the stomach for it but he stayed. He asked a lot of questions, kept himself talking. The coroner took zero chances with it. He was a thin, gaunt man, gentle in his work but not big on conversation. He answered Dyer's questions in short abrupt statements:

She passed between ten PM and two AM, he said.

She was eighteen or nineteen. No tattoos.

She'd had intercourse with multiple men the day before she died, one of them violently.

She abused intravenous drugs. They almost certainly killed her. "Stopped her heart dead," he said. "Everything else happened after."

"What about the wrists?" said Dyer.

"Handcuffs. That was before."

"You doing all the witchdoctor stuff?" said Harris.

"All underway. Dental, prints, toxicology. She had all sorts of things in her hair and nails. Skin, sand, leaves, blood of course, but also flecks of something else. Lots of it. I'm getting it looked at but I'm almost sure it's house paint. Smells just like it."

Dyer dropped Harris back at the house. "I've got another hour or two in me," he said. The garage door was open and Harris took himself inside. Roy was in his usual spot, up on a stool in his workshop, a black and white TV propped beside him on a milk crate. He had a bottle open.

"Bit of a long one for you blokes? Where's the boy?" he said.

"Working back."

Harris blew the dust out of a mug and took a pour.

"How bad was it?" said Roy.

"Pretty bad. Dead pro. I think we'll be on it a while.

There's no telling who she is. That's going to take a bit of doing."

Roy took his eyes off the television. "Don't let him get too mixed up in it if it goes the wrong way," he said.

"I'll do my best. But if he wants to go hard at it, I can't stop him. You know him."

"I never had that problem."

"What problem?"

"Wanting things."

"Ambition? Dedication?" said Harris.

"He must have gotten it from his mother," said Roy, with a shrug.

The late night news came on. They had a small piece on the scene. Jillian McMurty appeared. The medical officer's van drove past. They showed two other detectives canvassing a street. For one crisp moment, Harris saw himself. He and Dyer walked out of the bush land and onto the lip of the creek bed.

"He'll be glad he ironed the suit," said Roy.

Harris didn't say a thing. The image wasn't a good one. Anxious, hung over, pale, thinning hair. It was worse than the mirror.

"Wish I'd ironed mine," he said.

He looked away.

Harris went upstairs and called Cairns. It was late and Sarah Hannon still drifted in mind at this hour.

Sam Peters picked up.

"How is she?"

"They let her out yesterday," said Peters. "She seems good. As good as can be expected, I guess. They don't think she's going to try it again."

"Are they sending someone to talk to her?"

"They're sending someone," said Peters.

"She say anything to you about it?"

"Not a word. She keeps talking about coming back to work."

"You back in uniform?"

"Yeah," said Peters. "The vacation's over."

Harris let him go.

He took a beer and an apple from the fridge and went downstairs to the yard beside the flat. He lit a cigarette and stood for a while under the clothes hoist. Another hot, cloudy night. Harris felt his head swim a little as he sucked the smoke in. After a time he went inside and lay down, lit another cigarette, and put the apple on the nightstand. Harris managed to keep his eyes open long enough to tap out the smoke but he dreamed of fire anyway.

FRIDAY, FEBRUARY 8, 1985

HARRIS WAITED FOR THE visit all morning, and eventually Barry Caller came wandering in. He stepped onto their floor alone but Blintiff lurked in the building somewhere. Harris had watched them come across the street together.

"Better let me handle this," he said.

Dyer nodded. Dyer sat at a typewriter across the room, one hand bandaged. He typed slow, with the good hand. Caller actually smiled at him as he came in. Dyer looked away. He came around Harris's desk and sat himself on the corner, as if on a social visit.

"You called?" he said.

Harris turned over a photo of the body.

"Terrible business from what I hear," said Caller. "She looks young."

"Young enough," said Harris.

"On the job?"

"Probably. It's likely."

Caller put his hand on a photo, stared into it, totally undisturbed by the violence of the image. "I spoke to the coroner. This," he said, "this could be every girl we put the cuffs on in the last week. I figured as much." He removed a slip of paper from his jacket. "Your girl might be on here. If she is, let me know and we'll bring the right people to you. Hand delivered."

"I suppose you can't spare a man or two? We're a bit light on round here," said Harris.

"I'll be sure to mention this to the boys."

"I'd appreciate that," said Harris. "We might have to come over your side of town today and talk to a few people. Is that going to ruffle any more feathers?"

This was the purpose of the visit. There'd been an incident, thus Dyer's bandaged hand. As the kid told it, he spent the night in the city brothels asking after their Jane Doe. Earlier that morning, he had a bit of a run in with Jangles. Drunk off his ass and caught out, Jangles got overzealous with procedural jurisdiction and they got stuck into it. The fight didn't last long but they sent Dyer packing, rushed him home in someone else's squad car.

"I don't fancy leaving my car parked in front of a brothel for a second night running, is all," said Harris.

"It's all taken care of," said Caller. "Just keep your young friend over there…informed. We've got to play by the rules, Jim."

"I'll handle it."

Caller put his hat on and straightened the brim. On the way out, he passed behind Dyer and patted his shoulder. "No harm done, son," he said. "And tell your father I said g'day."

Dyer didn't look up from the typewriter. Straight-up anger played in his eyes.

Harris took it all in with a sense of unease. Matt Dyer was a star on the rise alright, but he had a lot to learn about office politics and policing. The kid knew how to look the other way but he didn't like looking directly around something in front of him, and that's what it took some days. That's what he'd need to learn to do if he was heading upstairs.

Dyer *was* smart enough to take free help, though. He ran Caller's list and got together a half-dozen names that fit the dead girl's description. Harris called down for the print work and made rough comparisons. None of them checked out but it didn't mean much. The licensing boys were known for taking the cuffs off someone for a favor. It was more likely that their victim was a known associate of one of these girls on Caller's list, one of these six who weren't in on The Joke. Dyer cross-referenced his notes from the night previous and ruled out three brothels. "No sign of her. No missing girls," he said, that left another two places as possible leads.

"So what have we got?" said Harris.

"You're not going to like it. The Palace and Summer Nights."

"Christ. That'd be right." The Agrioli family owned Summer Nights.

"You better be on your best behavior, Jim. You don't want to end up back in Cairns," said Dyer.

"Yeah, yeah," he said, but the thought of it churned in his guts.

The Palace was closed. They found the madam in the back yard, alone in knee-high grass, catatonically drunk at eleven in the morning. She was a ghost of a woman, all dark hair and white skin. She spoke in a slow, precise way but couldn't stand up from the kitchen chair she had herself planted in. "I get a little vertigo, darling."

Dyer stood beside her and said, "We're looking for a working girl. Any of yours missing?"

"Not that poor thing from Coopers Plains? That's a dreadful neighborhood. My ex-husband and I had a little place out there, by the army base."

"That's the one."

Harris wandered around the yard with a smoke.

"Let me think?" she said.

"Any of the girls quit? On vacation? Anything like that," said Dyer.

"Let me think." She sat there with blank eyes.

"Any—"

She shook her head, "No. They're all around."

"What about Denise Charters?" said Dyer, reading the name from his book.

"Denise is inside, I think. Why?"

"Our files show she was arrested last week."

Harris took in the whole view, the yard, the woman, and the near-dilapidated house they ran the brothel out of. It wasn't much of a knock-shop. Not one for the moneyed set.

"That's right," said the woman. "Denise went in."

"Why was that?"

"What does it say in your little book, darling?"

Dyer looked over at Harris. He shrugged.

"Solicitation," said Dyer.

The woman laughed a little. "You know, it's still a crime apparently."

* * *

Summer Nights was tucked away behind a nightclub in Fortitude Valley, not far from the club where Harris tussled with Roberto Agrioli. Set back from the road, the entrance was via a ramp leading off the street to an unmarked black door. Harris knocked and waited. Then he knocked again.

"We're not here to arrest anyone?" he shouted.

The door slid open.

A heavy Italian man stood in the center of a small reception area, every part of it glazed in pink light.

"This is subtle," said Harris, stepping inside.

"We're all square for the fortnight," said the man. "What do you want?"

They had decided on a different tack on the drive over. Dyer said, "We want to have a quick word with Fran. Is she about?"

"Always with Fran," said the man. "What is she ever done to you? You took her in last week. It was her turn."

"We just need to talk to her."

The man stared at them, one after the other, sizing them up.

"Okay," he said.

He took them through to a lounge area and told them to wait. The lounge was also furnished in pink. Pink satin on the chairs and cushions. Pink carpet. A pink coffee table. All topped off with a pink upright piano in the corner. The owners had a window cracked and the sun blazed in, revealing every gaudy detail.

"This is fucked," said Dyer. "If the rooms are like this, I'm not sure I could even get it done."

"You never want it to be too classy, if you're paying for it," said Harris.

They both heard the outside door open. A man came through. Harris caught a quick glimpse of him and had just enough time to say, "Oh shit," before Roberto ran across the room, raining fists. Harris brought his hands up. In the rush, Dyer managed to step in and lock Roberto, wresting him to the ground face down. The receptionist reappeared. He started screaming as well.

"You both need to fucking calm down," said Dyer, driving Roberto harder still in the pink shag pile.

"Get him to calm down," said Harris to the reception man. "Or he's going in. You're both fucking going in."

The shouting continued until the receptionist knelt down beside Dyer and Roberto and spoke in Italian. Roberto stopped struggling. Dyer let him loose.

"Stay down. Sit down, fuckhead," said Dyer. "Jeez, I guess this is the guy, right?"

"That's him," said Harris, rubbing his jaw.

Roberto took fast, heavy breaths. Dyer glanced around, still adrenalized. His eyes fixed across the room. Harris turned around and saw three women standing by the mouth of the hallway leading back to the rooms.

"Which one of you is Fran?" he said.

A spindly young girl with a mop of ginger hair nodded. "Yeah, that's me. But I've already had my go."

"Just get outside," said Harris.

Dyer pointed a finger at Roberto as they backed out. "You and I better not meet again any time soon."

They took Fran up to the pub and bought her a drink. Harris took a nip of scotch for his nerves and followed it with a beer. Even Dyer took a rare drink on duty. The girl didn't seem worried in the slightest. She sat by the window, lit a cigarette, and watched two council men work a sewerage manhole out on the street.

Dyer took down her info and asked the questions. No one was missing. The Agriolis ran a mean, tight operation. They rostered the girls on most days, for at least a few hours, and Fran — counting on her hand — had everyone accounted for.

"Sharon was sick two days back but I spoke to her yesterday. Jan left a month back, but she's pregnant. She'd be really pregnant now."

"How old are you?" said Harris.

Fran looked at him. "None of your business." She turned back to the street.

"Where you from?" said Dyer.

"Toowoomba. Came down last year after school."

"How'd you get started?"

"What is this? I just did, okay? They saw me at The Roxy a few times and then a friend of theirs spotted me on the job up near the laundromat, and one thing led to another. The way things are, I'm lucky to be there."

Harris knew the laundromat. Corner of Brunswick and Harcourt, strictly for the street girls.

"Here," Harris said and flattened a ten-dollar bill on the table. "Stay out of trouble."

"Sure thing," Fran said, sliding the bill across. "Can I go now?"

As they watched her come back past the pub window, Dyer shook his head. "I don't think I'm cut out for this some days."

"You're breaking my heart," said Harris. "Come on. Let's go and have a look up the road."

Harris figured their victim could be from out of town. Dyer followed the thought through: an outsider might explain the postmortem injuries. They could be an attempt to hide her identity. That would never work for a local girl, someone who'd be missed. "A street girl with no bludger, fresh off the bus," he said. "It adds up."

Harris agreed. "It's better than nothing."

At the laundromat, they found five girls on the sidewalk, each eyeing off cars and flicking their hair around. It was dusk. There were three cars banked at the lights, peak-hour traffic for Brisbane.

One of the girls must have been new to it. "You guys lonely?" she said as they crossed the street.

"Always," said Harris, getting out his ID.

The others started sighing theatrically. Half of them lit cigarettes, as if suddenly on break.

"Relax, ladies," said Dyer.

"We're looking for a girl. White, about five-eight, about eighteen, brown hair, thin. Missing for a couple of days. Sound familiar to any of you? I'm only going to pay one of you."

One of them stepped forward. "That bitch is gone back to Cairns," she said.

They all knew her, they said.

They called her Spiny.

Spiny said she was on vacation and needed money and a place to crash. The laundromat girls weren't too fond of the competition, but one of them had a spare room and needed a roommate. Ever since, the girl with the room had been whining about the rent owing. Harris bought the address for five dollars.

The place was a well-known shit heap down on Kent Street. Harris had seen a few bodies carted out of there in his time, ODs mostly. The girls living there tricked out of their apartments and got their junk home-delivered. As soon as they stepped out of the squad car, Harris could feel the building's workday grind to a fast halt. Curtains flicked open and closed. Toilets flushed. As they walked further in, Harris spotted two street urchins standing under a balcony sharing a joint. He knew them: the tall semi-retard was Whitey and the young kid next to him on the BMX bike was called Bandit. As they came up on them, Harris said, nice and loud, "I'm not going to find anything life threatening in number four, am I?"

Whitey was so spaced he didn't even stub out his joint.

"Nah. Nah, man," he said.

The little kid thought about it, then bolted.

They went up anyway. The woman who opened up looked drawn, tired, late thirties going on fifty. She was fucked up. She knew there wasn't much point pretending otherwise. "What do I have to do this time?" she said.

"Can we come in?" said Dyer. "I think we're looking for your roommate?"

The woman stepped aside. "Is that where she's been? With you two? She owes me money."

"Spiny, right?" said Dyer.

"She got a real name?" said Harris.

"I don't know."

Dyer pushed her gently back onto the couch. "What's your name?" he said.

"Linda."

"Full name."

"Chardy. Linda Jane Chardy."

Harris looked around. The front bedroom was definitely Linda's. She had her used fits resting in a bloody pile beside the bed and the whole room smelled like a hospital. Out back, Harris found a kitchenette and laundry. Down along the back wall, beside a bar fridge, lay a dirty mattress.

"She ain't leave nothin," said Chardy.

Harris turned the mattress up on its side. The smell of sweat and mildew wafted up. There was nothing underneath. He squatted down beside the bar fridge, where her head would have rested. In the cavity beside the compressor, he found a small cloth library bag. He spread the contents of the bag out on the tiles:

Two marijuana buds wrapped in foil.

Fifteen dollars in notes.

A pen knife.

A tattered copy of *Cujo*.

The book had a pile of photographs tucked inside. They were the smaller ones with rounded edges, family snapshots held together with a hair tie. Harris carefully took the band off. He felt cold, instant dread as he leafed through them. He laid them out in a grid and saw the same thing, over and over. They were younger and older, photographed together and alone, with different hair styles and clothes, but it was them. There were fourteen in total.

He felt the floor shift beneath him.

"You got something?" said Dyer.

Harris nodded.

He had ten photographs of Constable David Thompson, the kid who high-tailed it from the Cairns raid. Four photographs were of their victim. Same hair color, same build, same vibe. This would be her face.

Worst of all:

She was the girl Thompson ran from the brothel with.

I want to go with Laura.

"Fuck, that's got to be her," said Dyer. "Oh shit, that bloke's a copper. Look." He pointed to a picture of Thompson in uniform. "Any of this ringing bells?"

Harris stared at the photos for a few seconds longer then piled them back together.

"I don't know either of them," he said.

They took Linda Chardy in for further questioning. For two hours Dyer grilled her while Harris filed and prepped. He rang licensing, looking for Barry Caller. He wasn't in. Harris filed a brief for the Cairns police. From his desk, he phoned Sam Peters at home. It rang a dozen times before it connected.

She answered with, "Sam, is that you?"

Her voice. Sarah Hannon.

"It's Jim."

She hung up.

* * *

Harris walked to a service station he knew and bought a packet of cigarettes and a sly short-bottle of scotch. He took both back to the office and went up to the roof. They had an area up there, surrounded by an old sandstone parapet. It was where the higher-ups smoked. He had the place to himself. None of them worked nights. Harris took belts of the scotch and looked down the streets of Brisbane. Another sweatbox of a night. And now this, on top of summer.

He kissed the mouth of the bottle.

The door scraped open behind him.

Footsteps.

Dyer.

"Bum a smoke?"

Dyer lent back against the balcony. Yawned. Lit up.

"Anything?" said Harris.

"Not yet. Sounds like old Linda had a bit of a hard trot with the licensing boys so she's not saying a thing until one of them turns up."

"What do you think?"

Dyer shook his head. "I don't want their shit messed up with ours."

"Yeah. Well, we'll leave her over night. We might get lucky. She probably hasn't had a hit since late afternoon."

"She's already got the sweats."

"We're all sweating tonight," said Harris. "I sent that stuff through to Cairns. We'll probably hear later in the week."

"What about the bloke?" said Dyer. They'd talked

about David Thompson in the car back to the office. Dyer recognized his face, but nothing else.

"That's tomorrow's job."

"There must be someone rostered on who knows him. I can stay back, ask around?"

"It's fine," said Harris.

Dyer looked like hell.

"You need some sleep."

It was true. The kid was going too hard, too soon. But there was the rest of it as well. There was Dyer Senior and the Inspector to think of. And Barry Caller. The Palm Relaxo. Cairns. The girl on the beach. And more pressing was the next bottle back in the flat. Harris needed a lift home to it.

"Let's call it," he said.

SATURDAY, FEBRUARY 9, 1985

IN THE MORNING, a guard took them down to the holding cells to reinterview Linda Chardy. "We had to move her," he said. "I hope you two aren't taking this bitch anywhere, because she's a long way from presentable."

"She give you a hard time?" said Dyer.

"Not me, mate. But O'Dreary was on over night. He's not your biggest fan at the moment."

As they rounded the corner to her cell, the guard started cursing. Chardy had soiled herself and now lay face down on the concrete. The guard knocked hard on the glass window.

"Linda, I gave you a room with a toilet so you *wouldn't* shit on the floor."

"When did this happen?" said Harris.

"She's been sleeping it off since I came on shift, but *this*, this just happened."

Chardy stirred. She lifted her head off the ground and squinted at them.

The guard unlocked the food hatch and said, "You

chat with her. I need to go and get someone to come hose her off."

Dyer flinched as he put his face to the hatch.

"Linda?" he said.

She put her head back. "Where's the other guys?"

"They're not coming, Linda. You need to talk to us. What were you going to tell them?"

"Fuck off," she said.

"Come on, Linda. What does it matter? You talk to us, and you'll be home in a hour."

She started crying.

Harris felt the contents of his stomach rise. He took the handle of the food hatch and slammed it open and closed a few times. "Linda. If you have something to say, you better fucking say it because I'm happy to let you rot in there until you're spraying all over yourself from both ends. Whatever you have to fucking say, just say it."

"You can't do that?" she shouted.

Harris rattled the hatch again.

"Here comes the hose, Linda, fuck you."

She scrambled up. "No."

"What?" said Harris.

"She was looking for someone. That's why she came down here. That's all I know. She was in Brisbane looking for some guy. He's one of you cunts. She was going with cops to find him."

Harris looked down through the hatch, right into her eyes.

"Anything else?

They both heard her slump down against the steel door. Still weeping, she started mumbling to herself.

Dyer put his ear to the hatch and listened, shook his head. Then Harris closed her in.

They caught the first break an hour later. Dyer wanted to re-canvass the scene, a long shot in Harris's opinion, but on the way, they gave Fortitude Valley another pass. None of the working girls were out. Dyer took them down past Linda Chardy's motel. It was dead. No one answered their doors.

As they peeled back up Kent, Dyer hit the brakes.

"What about these guys?"

Up the street, two grubby kids jumped down the side of a fence and onto the sidewalk. One had a backpack. The other ducked behind a bush coming out the other side on a BMX bike. It was Bandit from the day previous.

"The one on the bike," said Harris.

Dyer got out and ran. Harris switched around to the driver's side and by the time he turned onto James Street, Dyer had Bandit by the hair. Harris left the ignition running and shoved a photo of the girl in the kid's face.

"You seen her? Look at it, dickhead?"

Bandit tried to nod.

"Let him go," said Harris. "Where?"

"Hooking. Round."

"What's her name?"

"Spiny."

"You drop stuff in to her?"

The kid looked up at Dyer. "Tell him, or you're definitely going in," he said.

"Sometimes," said Bandit.

"You seen her recently? Earlier in the week?"

The kid nodded.

"Where?"

"Out workin'."

"Where?"

"The laundry."

"You see her go with anyone?"

"Nah. She choosy. Mainly goes with you fellas."

Harris gave Dyer the nod and he let the kid go.

"Don't run from us next time," he said.

On the highway, Harris closed his eyes. Dyer listened to the radio. Neither of them talked about what the kid said. They didn't note it down.

Dyer drove back to the reserve and they trekked back to the bush land. Dyer had the maps and the aerial photos in a manila folder. He crouched down at the top of the long dirt hill that abutted the scene and opened the folder.

"My theory is, our guy didn't drive up here. If he did, he got exceptionally lucky," said Dyer. "So what if we scratch the whole idea that our guy came in the way we did. I've been looking it over and, look here… this other side of the bush land is serviced by, what is it, Candyapple Crescent."

"Who thinks up these names?"

"Some poof. Anyway, that's a no-go. Richo and one of those no-hopers from Vice did a few interviews yesterday and nothing, not a twig out of place in there the night in question. If they *find the time* today, they're going to do Bishop and Ferguson over here. I thought we might have a look at Peringa Street, here."

“That’s a long walk in,” said Harris.

“That’s what I want to have a look at. I haven’t been up this way.”

Dyer noted down the time, 10:42 AM.

They started off.

By 10:50 they were back at their car. Another three minutes got them to the houses adjacent to the reserve. Along the border of the park, a narrow asphalt path led down to a creek and a bridge. On the other side was another small park and further up sat an asymmetrical brick building with a small adjoining lot. Harris took a smoke break on the bridge. It was 10:52 AM. Then they continued up to the building, a community library.

“Maybe the librarian did it?” said Harris as they stood in the lot separating the park and building, his shirt wet with sweat. “Maybe our guy’s a book worm?” He’d had enough. The day started with his head in the office basin, removing it only to cop a mouthful from the Inspector (calling from Gatton) and then Linda Chardy’s shit-stained dress and now fucking Candyapple Crescent and the library.

“What’s the matter, Jim?”

“I’m not bouncing back like I used to. It’ll happen to you one day.”

“What do you want to do?”

“I’m going back to the office. I’ll try Cairns again, see if I can chase up Jane Doe’s name. I’ve got a two o’clock across the corridor to put a name to this copper from her photos.”

If Dyer spotted the lie, he didn’t show it.

Harris said, "I'll go back, radio for a lift. What are you doing?"

Dyer looked around. "This is all giving me the heebies." He had the map folded open and tapped it. "The main road is right there. It took us, what, fifteen minutes to walk to the scene from here, including a smoke break."

"You really think our guy could have marched her over there from here?"

"Our star witness went in there with some bloke, didn't she?"

It was true. Harris had seen enough bodies in enough places to know. Past a certain point, people will do anything. People will dig their own graves, silently, quietly, already dead but still hoping away.

Two patrolmen came for him, young blokes he didn't know. Harris had them stop at a pay phone on the side of the road. He phoned Barry Caller and left a message. "We need to meet up for a drink." He called a desk clerk he knew and gave her David Thompson's name and description. He asked the clerk to pull the file.

In the car, one of the cops smiled and said, "You know you can use our radio?"

One of them watched him in the rearview.

Harris rolled down the window and lit a smoke.

As soon as he got to the records desk, Harris could tell something was wrong. The clerk shook her head. "Jim, I can't release this to you. You better come round." She opened the side door and he went back. In a quiet corner, near a pile of typing papers, she said, "Thompson's file is off-limits. Word from above."

"This is regarding a homicide investigation. Is it all locked away?"

"What did this copper do?" she said.

"I don't know. Look, I'm going to see his C.O. after you. Do I really have to come back?"

"Don't bullshit me or you'll get the both of us into trouble with the old bloke."

"So the Inspector handed this down?"

"He did."

"Thompson is one of Barry Caller's boys," said Harris.

"Jesus," she said and walked.

He ran after her, "What?"

"You need to talk to Ann Masters. You're a fucking mess, Jim. Go and find Masters. I should never assume anything with you. You haven't spoken to her, right?"

"Why would I?"

"Do your job," she said.

The Pearl and Partner Hotel up on Wickham Terrace was out of walking distance for the Brisbane CIB. Its clientele consisted of ailing bar flies and off-duty queens. Senior Constable Ann Masters was not a fan. She held her glass of tap water up to the light and winced. "Silver service," she said. But she knew why they were there. Closed police files. A young constable. Not a conversation either of them wanted to have in earshot. Harris took a gulp of his beer. This wouldn't be good news. Ann Masters worked with broken coppers. That was her specialty.

"I'm looking for this guy," he said and spread two photographs of David Thompson out on the table.

Masters put her glasses on, took a harder look to be sure.

"What do you want?" she said.

"What do you mean, what do I want? This woman here next to him is our victim, still unidentified, in a homicide investigation. I need to talk to this copper."

"I'd like to talk to him too," said Masters. "But that's why he's on my desk. No one knows where Thompson is. He didn't report back to duty after leave last year."

"What do you mean? He's missing?"

"Yes and no," she said. "Stress leave. But, unofficially, he's in the final stages of getting himself booted off the force. That paperwork is winding its way up the ladder. He's about to become someone else's problem."

"But..."

"It might surprise you, Jim, that you have to actually turn up to work to be a policeman. He's been away for months."

"But why do you have it?"

"How much do you know about Thompson?"

"Next to nothing," said Harris.

"So you didn't run into him in Cairns when he was up there with Caller? You know, I was surprised when you rang. Are you sounding me out?"

"No," said Harris.

"You better not be. I don't want to get anymore tangled up in this than I already am. This is not me," she said. "This is something else."

Masters stood up. She took a long look at him and opened her purse. From inside, she took a small orange envelope.

"Take this and lose it."

"What is it?"

She thrust it into his hand. "Jim, for pity's sake."

Masters walked.

Harris went to the bathroom and opened the envelope. Inside was a postcard sealed inside a clear plastic evidence bag. On the photo side were two naked women. *Cum To Cairns*. On the back, scrawled in black ballpoint: I'M DONE. GOD HAVE MERCY ON YOU DOGS, D.T. It was mailed to Ann Masters at home. Harris checked the stamp. Postmarked Cairns, October '85.

He went back to the bar and had another beer. He waited an hour. He called Masters from the corner phone. She answered.

"Is this it?" he said.

"Everything else is in his file."

"Who closed it down?"

"You don't need me to tell you."

She hung up.

The weave of the corridor took its toll. Harris glided. He'd had one too many at lunch. Luckily, the place was deserted. He found his desk and tried Caller's line. Still no answer. He put a call through to Cairns and spoke with a desk sergeant.

"You get those photos I sent up? I'm still chasing an ID on the girl. I'm pretty sure she's from up your way."

The sergeant hadn't seen the photos.

Harris made a coffee and tried to sober up. The only

thing left to do was another canvass of the street corners. As the sun started to set, he chewed a stick of gum and went downstairs for a car.

Back at the laundromat, the girls were hard at it.

"Where's the other guy?" said a tall brunette in thick red stockings, despite the heat.

"He has a date."

"Too bad."

There were two new girls and Harris showed them the photos. They both barely glanced at them. They hadn't seen her. He walked down Kent Street to the flats and had another look around. On his way back up to the car, he saw a girl climb down from a truck cabin in heels. As she straightened herself up on the sidewalk, he approached.

"I'm a cop," he said. "I'm looking for this girl."

"Thought that looked like one of yours," she said, nodding at the unmarked.

He held the photo closer.

She shrugged.

As Harris crossed the street, she said, "I do cops on the cheap, if you're interested."

Harris had another look at her. She looked pretty good. Short but round in the bust, the tint of ginger in her hair and freckles.

She saw the pause. "What are you? Sergeant? Senior Sergeant?"

"Senior Constable."

"Senior Constable what?"

"Jim Harris."

"I like cops. You like girls, Senior Constable?"

"Don't." He looked up the street.

"No one cares," she said.

"It's not that."

She put a hand to his face.

She kissed him.

Her name was Birdy.

"Bye Bye Birdy. That's what they pay a girl like me for," she said. "You want me to leave?"

Harris stretched out on the bed. It was a dark room. He didn't want to see the rest but they were not alone. There was movement in the hallway, up and down, people coming and going.

Birdy ground herself against him, rocking back and forth.

"You want me to leave?" she said it again.

"No."

As Birdy worked harder into him, he could feel himself giving up. They'd been at it a while. It wasn't going to happen. Birdy noticed. She eased off. Eventually she stopped, laying her face down against his chest.

"Tell me a story," she said.

"Why?"

"Just do it."

"What do you want to know?"

She sat up and looked at him. "Why'd you become a cop?"

"Why did you become a pro?"

She laughed, "To stick it to my folks."

"Same," he said. "Not my greatest idea."

She sat up, "You get high, Senior Constable?"

"I've been known to dabble."

Whatever she had was potent enough. They smoked it off a piece of tin foil and it knocked him out for hours. When he found the energy to walk out of there, it was two AM. He found the car and drove a few blocks before realizing it was all too much to handle. Harris cruised down a quiet street and parked the car under a wide overhanging tree. He crawled into the back seat and passed out with the keys still in the ignition.

SUNDAY, FEBRUARY 10, 1985

THE SQUAD RADIO WOKE him. He let it go.

Harris got out of the car. The sun blazed. 9:35 AM. He knew the street. New Farm somewhere. He walked until he found coffee, then called home from a pay phone.

Roy Dyer answered. He said Matt was in a flap. A big night at the crime scene yesterday.

"You know where he is?" said Harris.

"Back out there, barely came in. He's been out there half the bloody night."

Harris ran back to the car . Out on the highway, he lit a cigarette. His hands shook like a heart attack.

Matt Dyer didn't say a word when he saw him. Instead he walked fast, taking Harris down past the Coopers Plains library to the bridge and creek behind it. Police crowded the creek bed, wading through the water and brush either side. Dyer's squad car was by the bridge, the trunk was open. He went to it and unfolded a bundle of plastic sheeting. "I had myself a nice little time yesterday," he said. "Took a walk by the water. Look what I found fifteen meters back from that bridge."

A claw hammer lay on the sheeting. It was well used, its wooden handle chipped and stained.

"In the water?" said Harris.

"Yeah, I figure he threw it in as he came past."

Harris checked the print dustings. "Anything?"

"There's a partial thumbprint. He didn't quite get the thing entirely under. We got lucky. They're running it now. I called it in. Been down here ever since trying to turn something else up."

"It's a bit of a long shot," said Harris.

"I reckon it's ours. I've got the science blokes pouring over the place looking for tire markings, anything. How'd you go with the copper in the photo?"

Harris told him about David Thompson and how he was on the way out. "He wasn't anywhere near Brisbane on the night our girl copped it. He's up north. The Cairns boys are trying to dig him up."

They walked down to the creek and talked to the beat cops. They'd turned up the usual: soiled underwear, food debris, a toy gun. Dyer let it run, handing the reins over to Richardson.

Back at the office, they submitted the hammer for testing and Dyer made a start on the paperwork. Harris made a show of calling around. The Cairns sergeant had another scratch about for the photos of the girl. He still couldn't find them. He called Sam Peters.

"Kid, I'm going to send you some photos. I'm sending them to your home address. Keep an eye out."

"A person of interest?"

"Victim."

"Mate, Cairns is small but it's not that small," said Peters.

"She's a prostie. You'll probably have paperwork on her. I just need a name. They call her Spiny down here."

"Doesn't ring any bells, but I'll keep an eye out."

Harris put the phone down.

"I'm going over to licensing," he said.

If Dyer wondered why, he didn't ask.

Barry Caller was out in Gatton but Harris found Blintiff in his usual spot. He was sitting back in his chair with his feet up, slowly rolling what looked like a meticulous cigarette. He held it up for Harris to see and said, "Why buy it when you can make it for cheap?"

They both lit up.

Blintiff scanned the room. "So, uh, what do you want, Harris?"

"I have a case open. A dead girl out in the suburbs—"

"I heard about that."

"Hold on," said Harris. He patted his jacket for the photo, handed it over.

"This her?" said Blintiff. "Christ. Not bad."

"The bloke next to her."

"Christ," he said. "Thompson?"

Harris nodded.

"That fuckhead is really in the bad books with Barry."

"What happened with him? You spoken with him?"

"Me? Christ, no. That kid was weak as piss. He was never going to hack it. Barry reckons he pulled the pin while we were still up north. I thought the kid was taking leave. Shows how much I know. That uptight bitch from the Missing Persons got a postcard from him, apparently."

Harris opened up his notebook and read, "I'm done. God have mercy on you dogs."

"Is that what he fucking said? Little shit. That's a bit rich. Good luck to him, I guess. If I could sit on some fucking beach in North Queensland, I would. If I could afford it."

"Maybe you can retire there one day?" said Harris.

Blintiff narrowed his eyes. He took his feet down off the table and pointed his cigarette. "Where I go after all this is none of your fucking business."

Harris waited a beat. "You know who the girl is?"

Blintiff didn't look at the photo a second time. "Fuck off. I'm busy," he said but he didn't move. He sat there and shook his head as Harris heaved himself out of the chair. As a parting shot, Blintiff called something across the room. It wasn't until Harris was in the stairs that he figured it out. Blintiff had told him to get some sleep.

Harris took the afternoon off. It was dark when he woke and the DTs were coming on. He walked up to the house for a beer and found Matt Dyer sitting at the kitchen table, the case file fanned out around him. He had all the trimmings. A list of known sex-offenders. A list of recent parolees. A list of previous murders and assaults with a similar MO. Canvass notes from the detectives. The crime-scene photos. Lab reports.

In the center of the pile was a photo of the victim and a list of possible surnames. He was looking for what Spiny could mean. He had Spinane and Spinner circled.

"Making any sense?" said Harris.

"Not really. It's a pile of nothing," said Dyer. "The boffins down in the lab reckon the hammer has been cleaned with a wire brush. That's their big bloody finding. That our guy has, sometime recently, cleaned the hammer, with a brush."

The kid looked pretty bad. He was starting to realize this would go south and he didn't look ready for it. Harris had seen it before. The ambition that got a man into homicide, especially a younger man like Dyer, that could bounce him out just the same. If this kid was ever going to have a career for himself — the career his father and his father's friends wanted him to have — they needed to get him through the CIB as fast as possible.

"She's a dead prostitute in the bush, mate," Harris said. "Those girls have a million different ways of getting themselves killed. And you never catch these blokes, that's the sad truth. This guy is probably going to just disappear back into the world. He's going to come and go. It happens."

"That's how I'm starting to lean with it," said Dyer.

Harris took a beer from the fridge. "So where to next?"

"I'm running these lists looking for someone who fits that kinda idea. One of these guys is a painter or a plasterer, has a car or a van or a truck filled with specks of paint and uses a hammer everyday. He's no fucking mastermind. He's not this copper we can't find up in Cairns. He's just some bogan dickhead, like a couple of these prize citizens here. Some of these blokes were in the vicinity in the last six months. I'm trying to narrow them down so we can go and have a chat tomorrow. See who fits and who doesn't. Sound okay?"

"It's how I'd do it," said Harris.

"You hear *anything* from Cairns?"

"Not a thing. They're on island time up there. But I know a guy who will move on it."

"Keep on them."

They sat for a time and looked through the paperwork. Harris crossed off names and added a few new ones. He knew some of these blokes from previous arrests. One had a knack for harassing street pros. Another had a string of rapes he'd greased his way out of.

Dyer worked until he started to nod off. Harris sent him to bed. When the house was quiet, he called a cab. As he waited out in the drive, he looked back at the house and saw Dyer Senior in the window. Roy stood there in a white singlet with the lights off, just watching the street. He waved and Harris nodded back. The old bloke kept odd hours. He seemed to never sleep. Said he wasn't capable of it most nights.

Birdy curled up next to him and brushed the hairs of his chest. Harris took another hit of the joint and ground it out. Everything about her smelled good. The shampoo in her hair, the scent in the laundered sheets, the weed like incense. She kept the place bathed in a low orange light.

"I knew you'd be back," she said.

"Did you now?"

"You get to know," she said. "I can tell."

Harris felt his mind wander. He took his cigarettes from his jacket and brought the photo of the girl out with it. He held the photo up above the two of them and stared at it.

"You find that girl yet?" said Birdy.

"Nope."

"She liked cops too, you know."

"Really? I thought you didn't know her."

"It's best not to know anyone when you're working. Spiny, right?"

"Laura," said Harris. "I think that's her real name. Laura Spinane, Laura Spinner, something like that."

"Yeah, Laura. I heard her called that."

"You see her last week, Birdy?"

"Just real quick."

"On the street?"

"Nah."

She yawned, on the verge of sleep.

"She just came past the corner is all. She always picked up this one john up further down the street."

"You remember the car at all?"

"It was a ute."

"What color?"

"Dark, gray."

"You sure?"

"Spiny owed one of the girls money and this girl was out. She saw her in the car and kinda shit-talked her as they came past. Threw her purse at the car and it bounced off the tray cover. No one liked Spiny. She was bad for business, and it's been a shit business lately."

"All the girls saw it?"

"Don't go getting me into trouble, Jim." She patted

his chest. "You go stirring things up and even I'll forget that I saw it."

Harris folded the photograph in half and slid it back into his jacket. He waited until Birdy started to snore before he gently moved her over. Harris lay there beside her until he felt himself starting to tire. Then he slipped out, padding down the hallway in his socks. On the street, he walked down to the Valley in search of a cab. It was a Sunday and everything was closed. He found a lonely-looking taxi parked in an empty rank. He knocked on the window and said, "Get me out of here."

TUESDAY, FEBRUARY 19, 1985

THE GATTON THING WRAPPED up. It wasn't neat but they found the guy and shot him. It read well in the press. One of the TV stations had footage of the CIB boys chasing their perp through a grain field. That was all anyone needed with a whole dead family in the picture. Case closed.

Detective Bill Crothers, always reliably left-of-center with his read on things, let out a long, tired sigh in the lunch room. "You know, it was a pretty good trip. They've got a good pub out there and our fine leaders weren't quite so tight with the O.T. On the whole, it was one of the good ones. Pretty good, I guess."

"But it worked, right?" said Dyer.

They all stood there.

Harris waited for it.

Crothers took a sip from his tea mug. "That bloke definitely killed them."

"But?" said Harris.

"Those kids were dead anyway. You should have seen the place. If our guy hadn't bloody shot everyone up, the parents would have starved or beaten those kids to death." He lowered his voice. "Let me tell you, the photos they're running of that smiling family in the paper, that's a decade ago. Our guy did the world a favor knocking them all off."

"What was it all about?" said Dyer.

The papers had kept their stories to the action.

"Fuck knows," said Crothers. "I've never seen anything like it."

Danny O'Shea walked in. He was Bill's partner. An old Irish bulldog of a man, violent but steady and ambitious. He opened the fridge and said, "Bill, when ya finished gas-bagging—"

"Fuck you, Danny," said Crothers.

O'Shea nodded. "Ow look, if it's nawt the night watchmen. How's it going, gents?"

"Fuck you, Danny," said Dyer.

O'Shea sniggered. "I heard ya caught yawselves a bit of a wee whodunnit in our absence. But I haven't seen ya in the paper recently? Ya need a hand or something?"

"Fuck you, Danny," said Harris.

"Ah, my work here is done," said O'Shea.

As they took their lunch back to their desks, the two detectives could feel it. The other men joked around, shouted across the room at each other. The office was riding high. The equilibrium was returning.

The Inspector, the one they called the Old Bloke, sat behind his desk like a government fixture. Round-shouldered and hunched, he wore a short, manicured haircut and thick glasses. Occasionally, Dyer mistook him for soft — Harris heard it in his tone — but the essence of the Old Bloke was solid brass. He was a wall Harris had bounced off before. At the desk beside him today was Barry Caller, and it was Caller who told them to sit down.

"Morning, sir," said Dyer.

The Inspector glanced at him and returned to a file he had open in front of him. A quiet minute ticked over. The Inspector cleared his throat and adjusted his eyewear.

"This is a bloody mess," he said.

Dyer leaned in. "I think that with a few more days, and some increased cooperation from the station up north, we could—"

"No, I don't think so," said the Inspector. "I don't. All you have here is a bunch of nonsense. While the rest of these men have been out there catching a killer, you two have been chasing your tails on a file that should have been sent my way a week ago."

"With all due respect sir, I—"

"He's right," said Caller.

Dyer had another go. "I think if we just…"

The Inspector kept on looking, right into Dyer. Dyer stopped speaking.

"Son, this is a pile of shit and I'm taking you off it. I want you to report to Detective Richardson immediately. For the next week, you're going to round up all the paperwork on this and have it sent to me. I'll tell Sandy to expect it. Just bring it to her desk. That'll be all."

"Sir, did I…"

"Don't wet your pants, Dyer," said Caller. "You don't want this shit dirtying up your trouser legs. He's doing you a favor. I suggest you take it."

"Out," said the Inspector.

Dyer got up and left.

As soon as the door closed, Caller walked around the desk. He sat beside Harris. He lit a cigarette and offered one to Harris.

"Don't even think about it," said the Inspector. "It's bad enough one of you smokes in here. I won't have two." He picked up the file. "Harris, you're starting to become someone I spend more time thinking about than I care to. And this," he waved it again, "this is a fucking headache."

"It was under control. The kid's smarter than he seems. There's only so much I can do to pull the reins without him noticing."

"What does he know?" said Caller.

"Everything and nothing."

The Inspector took off his glasses. He closed his eyes and began rubbing the spectacles on a handkerchief.

"What do you know?" he said.

"The young copper from Cairns, David Thompson, he's mixed up in it. Our vic was a pro. They were known to each other. He's gone. I'm no rocket scientist but I can add," said Harris. "I told Dyer that Thompson was in Cairns the night of the murder and we ruled him out, been running down other leads ever since. But I can't find much on that either way. And Dyer's right. Our Cairns brethren have been pretty fucking slack. As I said, though, I was keeping an eye on it."

"From what I hear, you've been drunk off your ass most of the time," said Caller.

Harris ignored it. "So what now?"

The Inspector turned to Caller. "Tell him."

"One of the brothel owners we have on the books saw Thompson down here the night of the murder. We've got a rental booked in his name at the airport, a white sedan, and our guy saw him pick up your girl on the night in question. Thompson was out of control. Had a bit of a habit before he joined the force, apparently, and got stuck back into it while we were in Cairns. He went off the deep end. He got mixed up with your bird, a Cairns local called Laura Spinane, nickname Spiny. I don't know what happened next but it knocked him for a six. Booze, weed, horse, the whole bit. We've been crossing our fingers that he'd come good. He didn't. A few weeks back, Spinane took off to Brisbane and he came after her."

The Inspector held up a photograph of Laura Spinane's body, "This looks like something a jealous idiot could do to a woman. Especially one hopped up on drugs."

"Except this idiot is one of ours," said Caller. "And if I let you and your partner keep yanking on these loose ends, things are going to get messy."

"Worse than it is already?" said Harris.

"A lot worse," said Caller. "It could get messy in a few different ways."

"Very messy," said the Inspector.

"Where's Thompson now?" said Harris.

They sat there a moment. The Inspector waved his hand, *proceed*.

"He left the country," said Caller.

"Left…the country?" said Harris.

Caller turned to face him square on. "Yeah. Permanently."

"Jesus."

"I can't have one of my men doing what he did, not when we're bloody well covering for him. You see our problem now," said Caller. "On top of which, none of us want Roy Dyer's son mixed up in this. So he's going to tell you what's going to happen and you're going to do it."

"I want to stay on the right side of this," said Harris.

The Inspector nodded. "Good. Well, this is the end of it then. It's going to go like this." The Inspector began to speak in his quiet, measured way. As he laid out the story, Caller interjected details and ideas. Together the three of them got it worked out, and for the most part they were right. Caller and the Old Bloke had a good read on what could be done. They had the pull and the connections. They were both masters of sliding an agenda through and keeping everyone happy along the way. All Harris had to do was let it happen and keep his mouth shut. And in all the machinations and back-channeling and corruption that these two men summoned, Harris's role — or lack thereof — seemed like nothing at the time, an afterthought.

PART THREE
PURGATORY
1985

WEDNESDAY, FEBRUARY 20
TO
SUNDAY, NOVEMBER 10, 1985

THE CITY STARTED TO fall and the rest of '85 passed like a fevered dream. They made a fast promotion out of Dyer, got him up above the waterline.

"Up where he can do naw harm," said O'Shea.

Harris knew better but he said nothing.

Dyer took the gift. He had to. They had him round up the case files for Laura Spinane's murder and deliver them to management. After a few directives from the Inspector, Detective Richardson took the enquiry down a different path. The lab work from the Gatton murders came in and there were correlations, a lot of matching components between that case and the hammer found in the creek. The drug murders of Gatton were the work of a lone gunman and within a fortnight of reassigning Dyer and Harris, the brass had rolled the two cases together. The Gatton killer, it seemed, also beat Laura Spinane to death while on the run, and what everyone in the department heard as a joke — a story that no newspaper would print — the city swallowed whole, without hesitation or pause. From the comfort of his desk and the bar and a series of slow, anonymous cases, Harris watched it all come and go. He kept his mouth shut, as promised. He waited for his reward.

Things changed a little at home. Matt Dyer found himself an apartment closer to the city. Harris stayed behind with Roy Dyer. Each night they took their drink in the garage by the television, until winter drove them upstairs. Every now and then he did what he could to help Roy with the house, but the old man wasn't much for clean living. It never went over well with the old copper.

Roy remained eternally grateful that his son had survived CIB without demotion. To Roy, there was only one game to play in the force and he'd found a coach for his son in Harris. That's how he saw it and Harris couldn't disavow him of the notion. "I didn't do much," was all he'd ever say. He didn't want the gratitude, or the blame.

It wasn't exactly a good moment for Matt Dyer. Harris knew enough about people and their problems to read it in Dyer's eyes. The kid knew what he'd been part of, if not the exact details or design. A lot of unhappiness played out in him openly after the promotion. He fell quickly out of shape. He had a paunch by August of that year. Harris could never find the words to put it right. He had no talent for talking people round and the truth remained: it wasn't right.

So Harris stood aside. He watched a dubious part of his career unfold and surprised himself with mixed feelings. He had to fight the urge to dwell on the Spinane case, as if his mind wanted to relive it. This was a reaction that made no rational sense to him. She was just another dead body. She was gone. But something of her lingered.

Drunk one night, he stood on an overpass and watched the cars below. He let his mind have its way. He zeroed in. There was something about the young David Thompson that felt familiar, as if their fates were joined. It was ludicrous. Superstitious, almost. Harris laughed with a force he knew was bordering on manic. He flicked his cigarette down onto the highway below.

The following day, he woke up in the long grass of the yard, laid out under a blue tarp he could barely remember crawling under. As he lay there, Harris figured — as he often did that year — that this would be the last of it: just another bad night, of which there was a dwindling supply. It would fade.

And yet it didn't. The creeping fear kept building, and Harris never said a word of it to anyone.

There was no point.

There wasn't a way to pull it all together.

The dark gray utility vehicle that took Laura Spinane.

The fact she was looking for Thompson in Brisbane, not vice versa.

Thompson's missing person file.

The little girl at the Cairns brothel who knew Laura.

Sarah Hannon halfway dead in the hospital.

The history between them. The connections.

His father. The stuff worse than his father.

His brother, worst of all.

Lachlan.

The stories played over and over, and the reason for their constant return never presented itself that year.

There was nothing to say. There was no reason to tell a soul. There was nothing left to do but drink and live it out.

The one glimmer in the shit pile was Birdy. She seemed like such an afterthought during the tail-end of the Spinane thing. She grew larger and larger in Harris's thinking as '85 dwindled on. Nothing concrete changed: She still worked, she still drugged, she still drank. But over time, she became a part of the year and part of him. That spring, in particular, she was everything. As the squalor of their time together hit an all-time low, Birdy found a way to the crux of it.

One night, they tried their hand at needles and, like an answer to all confusion and turmoil, heroin cut through like a laser. They took it easy. Harris had to work (a small, nondescript trail of textbook suicides and dead elderly) and Birdy had to trick. They made a rule of once-a-week for a few months until that collapsed into twice-a-week and that's how it went, right through till the end, right through to the night in November where Harris came to on the floor and spat vomit across the rug beside him.

He woke in the hospital.

Matt Dyer stood beside the bed.

His throat hurt. He couldn't speak.

"The girl's dead," said Dyer. "They found her crumpled in a heap beside you."

Harris rolled over and wept.

Sarah.

Laura.

Birdy.

All because of him.

All with him.

All staying with him now till the day he died.

The Inspector called later that same night and a nurse took him out to the phone. "I'm transferring you," he said. "I want you out of Brisbane for good, you stupid bloody clown. When you get yourself out of there, don't even come into the station to clean out your desk. Don't bother. You're done here. The moment you're up and walking, you put yourself on a plane. I don't care where the hell you go, just stay there until the day you do us all a favor and quit. You hear me? Or do me a big favor and quit now? You hear me, Harris?"

He stood there.

The silent hallway. The nurse beside him.

Harris said nothing.

The Inspector screamed, "Are you fucking listening to me?"

Nothing.

He turned the receiver in his hands.

"Answer me, Harris, or there will be worse to come. Mark my words."

He felt tears, warm lines on his face.

The nurse looked terrified. She patted his back, and Harris stared at her and felt the whole thing cave in.

"Cairns," he said into the telephone, at last. "Send me back to Cairns."

PART FOUR
CAIRNS
1986

MONDAY, NOVEMBER 11, 1985
TO
WEDNESDAY, JANUARY 15, 1986

SAM PETERS PICKED HIM up from the airport and drove him into town. The department paid for a full relocation. It didn't cost much. They set him up in a rundown whiteboard motel on the second floor, a street back from the ocean. The place was near-on empty: a retired couple on the ground floor, the landlord's flat beside them. Peters didn't hang around. The place gave him the creeps.

That evening, Harris walked down to the beach and stood beneath the pink sky. He opened a fresh pack. As the water lapped at his ankles, he took a short-bottle of whiskey from his pocket and washed down a half-dozen smokes.

Back to this.

When he woke, he was back in the motel, sand on the carpet. The phone was ringing.

He picked it up.

"Hello?"

The caller breathed into the handset.

"Say something."

Nothing.

Harris put the phone down.

Bad news traveled fast.

He went to the station house and it was exactly the same. They gave him the same desk, in the same hallway. The same lamp bulb still needed replacing. This was it. The long trek to retirement.

The rest of November and December rolled past. The Senior Sergeant in Cairns, Ryan McArthur, played it civil but nothing more. He had his own detective by then, a new bloke McArthur trusted and who was smart enough to refuse a gig with Harris. Instead, Harris worked two break-and-enters — both unsolved — and took notes on a kitchen fire. For the most part, he sat in his office with the door closed, his head in a paperback novel or a bottle or adrift in history. He only occasionally saw Sam Peters, more often than not at a pub. The kid was around. He wasn't going anywhere either.

The late night phone calls kept coming.

Harris knew this was it this time. It didn't matter who was on the other line or what the world thought of him. He was home now and all the ghosts were interconnected. They all knew where to find him. They were *all* calling. And they all had the same body.

He waited.

And eventually she came.

It was New Years Eve, 1986. Harris watched the fireworks explode through the venetian blinds. He sat in a chair by the window and he'd been there for hours. His bladder ached. He peered out, watching the pink and green flames flicker in the sky and trail down across the window glass of the cars opposite. That's when she appeared, like an apparition. A solitary character standing still in the crowd. She leaned back against the trunk of a sedan, the ember of a cigarette glowing. She was watching the place.

Sarah Hannon.

She must have seen the blinds, his hand. Hannon stubbed out the smoke and came across, the sound of her heels making a dull drone on the stairs as she walked to his room.

And then the knock came.

Harris sat there and stared into space.

"Why?" he said to himself quietly.

He opened the door.

"Happy New Year," she said.

She looked drunk as hell. He felt the same.

"What are you doing here?" he said.

"I was always here," she said and pushed past him.

He gave himself to her. He went to work. He went to the pub. He came back to the motel and he let her in. The nights she didn't come, she called. Her marriage hadn't survived his last visit, nor the baby she finally got round to mentioning.

"I don't know if it was his or yours. Yours, probably," she said. "We'd been trying and I was sure I couldn't get it done. They told me I couldn't, a long time ago. And they were right, I guess."

"Why didn't you just get rid of it?" said Harris.

"I did get rid of it."

"You didn't need to hurt yourself."

"Yes I did. You're one to talk. You should try it. I think you'd really take to it. A good suicide attempt might be the best thing for you, Jim. It did me the world of good."

Spooked, he locked himself in the bathroom and waited. An hour later she was gone. On the wall above the bed, she had scrawled a single word in red lipstick:

LACHLAN.

He stared at it.

He let it wash through him.

The true beginning. All the carnage led back to this.

The booze raged in him. He hurled on the motel carpet. Squeezed tears out of his eyes. Harris unclenched his fist and saw white.

Hannon was right:

It was time to take himself out of it.

THURSDAY, JANUARY 16, 1986

THERE WAS NO CLEAN slate in the morning. Harris stepped out of the motel into gray summer rain, humid like a sauna. The repetition pummeled him like waves:

The weather.

The city.

The bottle.

Hannon.

A year down the toilet. No change. Back to this.

He caught a cab to the station.

Harris locked himself in his office and cleared his desk. He remembered the bottom-drawer whisky and took it to the car park under his jacket and poured it down a storm-water drain.

He called Hannon and woke her.

"I'll give you what you want," he said. "But only if you stay the fuck away from me."

"It was just an idea," she said. "We'll see."

He made a pact with himself.

Get the answers.

Raise hell.

Then give the world what it wants.

If he played his cards right, they'd kill him before he had any say in it.

He made two dossiers.

LACHLAN

LAURA

He started them fresh, ran clean sheets through the typewriter. He made the routine searches.

Two days disappeared into it.

He started two charts on the motel-room wall. Harris looked at them.

The last cases.

"And my first," he said later in the night, gasping for air.

Sarah came on the third night.

She didn't care what he wanted. She didn't explain herself.

"This looks interesting," she said, after.

He had retained the lipstick-smudged LACHLAN and ran two pinned lines out from the word to the first pieces. A librarian found them for him in the local archives. LOCAL MAN DISAPPEARS and SEARCH CONTINUES FOR MISSING SPORTSMAN. Both from *The Post,* both ran with a photo: Lachlan Harris, aged twenty-six.

"You look just like him now," said Hannon.

Harris grabbed her.

She acted cool but in bed, she refused him any way that obscured her view of LACHLAN. She stared at the wall as she leaned over him. When it was done, she got dressed back into her uniform and turned the lights on.

She read the other chart and said, "This looks like trouble."

"That's what it is," he said.

She stared at him. "I broke the deal."

He shrugged, "I don't think I really made it with you."

She turned back to the LAURA chart and said, "I knew Thompson, off and on. I remember him. I heard he quit. You know, he looks a bit like you, too. This is a nice little house of mirrors you've got going here."

He took her by the arm and threw her out.

Harris had to be careful with the file searches. The licensing boys and the Inspector seemed to have a knack for the paperwork. They knew people. Harris didn't want any red flags going up.

Not yet.

He had Sam Peters run up a dummy case file, a hypothetical kid — high as a hypothetical kite — claiming he killed a bloke in January 1985. Harris mocked up a set of prelim notes, marked the thing as a hoax and sold it to the Senior Sergeant. "I might run the files anyway, see if anything jumps out. Just in case," he said. The Sergeant didn't give a fuck. So Harris ran it all out, 1980 to present and got a list of every body on the books. The history of Cairns as a bad place.

It was a long list. But an hour with it was all it took. He didn't even have to try. The thing was lying there right open, in plain sight.

December 19th, 1969: Frank Thompson, dead, overdose, David Thompson's father. He pulled the file. Frank Thompson had never taken a pill in his life. The night in question, he had enough of them in his bloodstream to kill an ox. He checked the scene photos and found mayhem and shitty policing. Frank was beaten before he died. *Self-inflicted wounds to the head and throat.* Frank's body was moved, by the looks. Frank was a frame-up. The investigating officer: Ray Blintiff, on loan from Brisbane CIB.

Harris went to the storeroom and unbagged Frank Thompson's effects. They had it all, a torn shirt, the pill bottles, a note. He opened the dead man's wallet and pulled out a photo: Frank as a young man, with two kids and a woman sitting either side of a plastic tree and wrapped presents. He flipped it over: *David, Laura and Jenny, Christmas 1966.* He flipped it back and stared into it. History went off like an atomic bomb in Harris's mind.

David and Laura.

Brother and step-sister.

Both of them looked like the woman. Siblings with a different surname.

Harris dragged over a steel bin and puked.

He trawled back through the paperwork and found the wife in the photo.

Jennifer Spinane.

Deceased also, suicide also, 1968. Spiny and Thompson, two orphans in the space of a year. Queensland Police everywhere, all over it.

Harris filed through their story. They were raised in Gordonvale, in the south. He knew the place. Cane country. The family estate.

He drove out. It was a house on stumps jutting out of the crop line. Driving up to the homestead, Harris felt the buzz. He knew these people. These were people who kept to themselves. They sat on their history.

He parked under a tall orange tree. A tractor came past in the field adjoining. Harris waved. The old man behind the wheel held his middle finger up and spat.

"Don't mind him."

The voice came from the house. A woman stood on the porch in shorts and slippers, rollers in her hair. She watched the tractor drive further into the distance.

"That your husband?" said Harris.

She nodded. "He don't like anyone from the government much. Those property fellas have been out here hiking up the rates. And he's getting blind. You don't look like a property fella to me. You look like a policeman to me."

"I'm looking for Ann Spinane."

"Yeah, that's me," she said.

"I want to talk to you about your granddaughter, Laura."

She looked through him for a moment and said, "Do you, now? Well, you better come in."

Ann Spinane sat him at a Formica table in the kitchen and made tea. She took a sponge cake from the pantry and insisted he take a slice. "You look like you could use it," she said.

"I'm new in town," said Harris. "I worked on your granddaughter's case in Brisbane."

"They caught the fella who did that, didn't they?"

"They did. I'm just following up a few loose ends."

"Is that what Laura was?"

She didn't look across when she said it. Instead, Ann Spinane stirred a spoonful of sugar into her tea.

"I knew her brother, David Thompson. I worked with him briefly," said Harris. "Do you know where he is, Mrs. Spinane?"

"No one knows where David is. He could be dead for all we know. He left us all years back."

"When was the last time you saw him?"

She stirred some more, "Let me see, I haven't seen David in probably ten years. Maybe more."

"What about Laura?"

"No. We weren't a close family."

"I think they both got mixed up with some of the wrong people up here. I'm trying to piece together a bit of a timeline, see if I can work out how some of this might have happened. The case in Brisbane doesn't really add up."

"It's a bit late for that, don't you think?" said Spinane.

"Better late than never," he said.

She sighed. "What do you want to know?"

"Tell me about them."

Ann Spinane moved over to the sink and lit a cigarette. She blew the first lungful out the window but didn't fuss with the rest of it. As the details flowed out of her, Harris felt himself fade out. He could feel the loneliness of her, a woman who had buried two generations, daughter and granddaughter.

"Bloody Frank," she said. "He was pure garbage, right from the start. All the Thompsons were, except

David. Frank swooped on in and snatched Jenny up when she was seventeen. She was damned pregnant by another man, silly girl. The other guy didn't want it so she had to settle for Frank. She was too young. She had David before she'd ever worked a job or drove a car or any of that. It ruined her, I reckon. She was stuck. And bloody Frank knew it, too."

Harris almost switched off as the old woman told the next part. Frank as a bad man. Frank as the interchangeable face behind so many dead daughters and sons, the figure in the background of too many cases he'd worked. Frank as the man Harris had met over and over again:

A stone drunk.

A pathological bully.

Randomly violent and chemically fucked.

Dangerous.

The kind of man that makes junkies and head-cases and predators out of his children, or someone else's. Prostitutes and policemen, too.

"Our Jenny didn't stand a chance," said Ann Spinane. "He would have killed her if she didn't beat him to it."

"Why'd Frank top himself?"

"Boredom, I'd say. I always figured he killed himself when there was no one left to push around. We took the kids after Jenny died. No courts, no nothing. We just went and got them. The police — for whatever you blokes are worth — at least backed us on that."

Harris saw the tells every now and then, but they came clear at the end. Ann Spinane was a terrible liar.

Frank was no lonely suicide.

She'd seen David Thompson recently.

There was more.

Harris stared at the LAURA chart on the motel wall. The grandmother's vibe spelled collusion and survival-at-all-costs. Harris had the property files of their farm. He checked for hiding spots. They had a cabin in the backfields. They owned real-estate, a rental house in Whitfield.

Harris put himself in the frame. Stared at a picture of Laura and thought it through.

Junkie.

Prostitute.

He stared at a photo of David.

Policeman.

Cairns escapee.

Brother.

"If I was you," he said, holding up Thompson. "And I found you—" the photo of Laura "—working at the Palm Relaxo, I'd take you home," said Harris.

No surer bet: David Thompson went back to them. They had what he needed. He had their granddaughter. But it would disrupt things. Whatever it disrupted got them both killed.

And yet families rescue their daughters from the game all the time. There had to be more to it.

It all went back to Laura.

Junkie.

Prostitute.

Granddaughter.

And something else.

* * *

Someone had painted the Palm Relaxo but it still looked pretty bad. Harris waited in the dark, listening to the rain bucket the car's roof. When it eased, he went over. The door opened on an older woman, mid-fifties, big. She filled out a red cocktail dress like poured concrete.

"You got an appointment, pal?"

"It's been a while," said Harris. "I used to be a regular about a year ago. Used to go with Laura. She in?"

The woman unlocked the screen.

"Come and have a drink, mate."

Three girls waited in the living room. All wore the same red cocktail dress. The woman fixed whiskeys. She took a long pour for herself.

"You a local, love?" she said.

The girls looked at Harris.

"Used to be. Back for business."

"What's your name?"

"Call me David."

"Now, David, Laura doesn't work here no more but I'm sure one of these girls can give you what you're after. Isn't that right, girls?"

This was the room Caller and Blintiff had everyone laid out in during the raid.

"It's a bit different," he said, looking around. "New management?"

"Something like that, darl. I wasn't here last time you came by, was I?"

"No. I would have remembered someone like you."

She vamped it up. "If you ever had me, doll, you'd remember." She laughed and her cackle sounded borderline psychotic. Harris laughed with her. He took a gulp of his drink.

The woman said, "Up, up, up," and the girls slowly got themselves to their feet. They pirouetted. One stared straight through him. The rest looked distracted, medicated. Harris picked the one least like Birdy, a small brunette with long arms and legs. The rest were dismissed. The three of them sat together in the room and had another round. They made bad, stilted smalltalk. Eventually the thin girl took him through to a room and said, "You better have a shower?"

"Sit down," he said and closed the door.

He opened his wallet and dropped two items on the mattress:

His police ID and two hundred dollars.

"I just want to talk. The police station or right here. Your choice, but one of them pays better."

"Talking's worse than fucking," she said. "Or is it one then the other."

"Just talking," said Harris. "So you may as well take the money."

"That depends on what I have to say."

He took out Laura's photo. She looked at it.

"Spiny," she said.

"Tell me about her."

The girl went to the bed and took the money, "She was okay. Been in the game too long. It fucked her up. She went to Brisbane, last I heard."

"You work here with her?"

"Yeah. Off and on. She only pulled shifts here on the sly. She was with the brothers then. You're not supposed to go your own way when you're with them."

Harris held the photo closer. "Tell me about these brothers."

"The brothers own everything now. They're the only game in town. They took this over a year back."

"What are their names?"

She huffed, "You aren't much of a detective. Sienna. Sal and Al Sienna," she said. The name sounded familiar. "That's all I'm saying for two hundred. You need to wait a while before you leave or I'll get in trouble."

Harris picked up his ID, "Is there a little girl living here?"

"We don't do that sort of stuff."

"No, just living here."

She shook her head.

Harris sat down and lit a smoke. The girl bummed one. They waited.

"I hate the rain," said the girl as she stared out the window.

Back at the motel, Harris's mail sat by the door. Five more clippings for the LACHLAN chart. They all showed his brother's sporting prowess, local wins. They were more than that, though. They were locations, away games, dates.

Harris put them up.

He worked late.

Hannon stayed away.

He let himself drink a short bottle and it hit him hard.

He was getting tired.

MONDAY, JANUARY 20, 1986

SAM PETERS SAT ACROSS the booth from him in the milk bar and frowned.

"The Siennas?"

"That's right," said Harris. "What do you know about Sal?"

"He's the dumb one, Al Sienna's idiot brother. A rough nut."

"What are they into?"

"Well, Al's a real estate shonk, or was. Years back, he made a killing off land up the coast, half of it underwater, sold it off the plan to overseas dupes. Nearly went down for it too, but he managed to grease the right palms. Everyone else copped it. One of the local blokes lost his seat and one of the cartographers is still in the clink. But his brother, Sal, Salvatore, he was small time. Ran some local girls, gambling, and for a stretch he was a regular guest in the watch-house. Loved a drink and punch on. He was a boofhead, I guess.

"Was?"

"The talk is Al shipped him home. Got to be too much."

"When was this?"

"A year back, maybe more."

"You know anyone on that side of things who'll talk?"

Peters wrote down a name and address.

"Maybe. But don't piss her off, mate," said Peters. "She's a doctor."

Harris paid the bill.

He followed the Al Sienna lead first. The brothers were incorporated; they had an office in Palm Cove. It was closed, 11 AM, Monday morning. They had brochures out and Harris took one back to the car. They had land for sale, *Come To Turnell Island*. There was a map. The island was a long way down, halfway to Brisbane, just off the coast of Rockhampton. The Siennas could sell you a house-and-land there for fifty-five thousand dollars, no down payment. You could time-share a *Luxury hotel suite with water views! A quick drive from the mainland!* Buy in, get rich, live easy. There was a diagram: they were building some sort of tunnel over to the place. It looked like science fiction. And it looked big, too big for a couple of crooks from Cairns.

Harris turned the brochure over and checked for a phone number. Right there, the size of a postage stamp, was a picture of Alessio Sienna.

It hit Harris like a punch.

"*You see out there, that's the future, Detective. And this is how it feels, like a blow job from a young girl.*"

The Italian from the beach.

The night out with the licensing boys.

The center point.

The Siennas, and Barry Caller's breed of police. This was bad. Whatever happened to Thompson and Spinane, they got themselves caught up in the gears of this.

Sam's informant was no down-and-outer. She lived in a high-rise apartment on the foreshore. "I don't need to know who you are?" she said, waving him in. "I owe Sam a favor but not a big one. So don't overstay your welcome."

The usual line.

She went to the balcony and pulled the blinds.

In the dark, she looked like Harris felt. At the end of something.

"I need help with a case," he said.

"Nope. I'm a doctor. I…I do things for people who need them. I don't help policemen," she said. "So you need to be more specific."

Harris took out a photo of Laura and showed it to her.

She recognized her; it showed.

Harris took one of her cigarettes and lit it. "I know she was hooked up with Sal Sienna. I know she worked as a prostitute. And I know she had a shitty father up here and that her brother, David, was a cop in Brisbane, using his mother's maiden name, Thompson. She's dead now, a year back, in Brisbane. But I want to know why she left Cairns."

The doctor put the photo down. "Why does anyone leave Cairns?"

"To get away from the people who live here. Did you treat her up here?"

"I treated her."

"Why?" Harris opened his wallet. He took all the cash he had and put it on the coffee table.

"Tell me everything," he said. "I'm a person who needs something."

The doctor picked up the money and counted it.

"Sal Sienna brought her in. She worked for him, but I think they were closer than that. Sal didn't bring the other girls in. Laura was a fucked-up junkie hooker. Totally incurable."

"Why was he looking to get her cured?"

"What do you know about AIDS, Detective?"

"Not much."

"It's a disease of the immune system, it shuts you down. It's going to be a big deal. It's going to hurt a lot of people. You get the flu, you die. You get a cold, that's it, show's over. It's in your blood. People get it from swapping blood or fluids, so intravenous drugs, unprotected sex…"

"Needles?"

"Yeah."

"And Laura had it?"

"She either had it, or something just like it. She was sick. Did your people do an autopsy?"

He nodded.

"And?"

"I don't know," said Harris. "I don't think we ever got the full report."

"Wow. And a year later, here you are," she said. "Are you okay?"

The brunt of it had taken a few seconds:

Birdy and Laura worked the same corner.

Birdy and Laura could have shared their drugs. Or the same john, just once.

Whatever was in Birdy's blood was in Harris's blood.

He felt himself run cold. Sweat broke through his skin like a flood.

"What's this got to do with the rest of it?" he said.

She laughed, "Who *are* you?"

"I don't know," he said. "I don't know."

"You look like shit." The doctor went to the kitchen and opened a drawer. "You want to stay awake or go to sleep?"

"Awake," he said.

She tossed him a box of pills. Dextroamphetamine. "Don't take too many of those. And I need you to get out now. You don't need me. You'd be better off without all this. If it helps you sleep at night, a lot of these men around her, maybe even the guy who killed her, they're all going to die. No one could save this girl. Not you, not me. Not her brother. No one. The whole thing's finished, the way I see it. Or it's going to be, soon enough."

At the door, Harris said, "Did you see David Thompson when he was up here?"

"He came to me. His sister needed some things. He knew all this."

"How'd he take it?"

She nodded at the wall across from her doorway. A plastered-over fist-sized hole sat in the plasterwork.

"How do you think," she said.

The door closed.

Harris looked at the busted wall.

He stared into the hole and suppressed a scream.

He drove to the hospital and had a blood test. The nurse knew a bit about the virus. He asked her straight up, "Can I pass this on to a woman if I used a rubber?"

He always used one with Hannon. There was no trusting her after last time, after the baby.

"Not really," said the nurse. "It's rare, apparently."

"How rare?"

She stared, got a good read.

"Wait and see how this turns out first."

She told him to wait for four days and call back.

Harris spent the afternoon trawling the brothels and dives. No one had seen Sal Sienna in months. He'd disappeared. "He went home," said one of the girls. Harris went to the station and checked the files: no arrests or appearances since December '84.

He rang the airlines and had them run searches on both brothers.

Al Sienna hadn't left the country in years.

Sal Sienna had booked himself on a flight to Rome, January 20, 1985.

He rang the doctor back.

"When was the last time you saw Sal Sienna?"

She laughed, "You're getting the hang of this, Detective."

"When?"

She turned pages. "Mid-January."

"What sort of shape was he in?"

"No comment."

"Could he fly?"

"He didn't fly anywhere."

Harris did the math.

About three days after David Thompson rescued his sister, Sal Sienna — Laura's pimp, Laura's boyfriend — goes missing.

"Who did it?" he said.

"The person you think."

She hung up.

Sal Sienna: thug, ladies man, dealer, AIDS carrier. Something like that. Murderer, perhaps. Harris went to the chart and marked it: *presumed dead.* Two missing brothers, both sides of the fence.

Tit for tat.

It was where this was heading.

Later:

The two charts.

Harris stood between them, naked, a bottle in hand.

He took long drags and the dexies ran their course.

Harris had the street directory, Al Sienna's coast-side home circled in ragged ballpoint.

The phone rang. He let it go.

Harris pumped himself up.

Four days.

It was enough.

Four days to get this finished.

Four days to get complete.

Redemption.

Or punishment.

They had a test for it now.

PART FIVE
FOUR DAYS
1986

Day 1:
TUESDAY, JANUARY 21, 1986

IT WAS DARK. THE rain bucketed down. Harris drove through it. Two miles out from Sienna's manse he spotted a deserted phone box and rang Matt Dyer in Brisbane. Through the roar of the storm, he shouted, "I'm coming back!" He could feel himself slurring. "Get everything you can on the licensing squad, especially Caller and Blintiff. Do it tomorrow! Do it on the quiet!"

Dyer was half asleep. He started to argue.

Four days.

"Do it tomorrow, or you go down with the rest of them," said Harris.

Dyer sighed, "What the hell, Jim? Are you okay?"

"Just do it."

"Okay," said Dyer.

As Harris put the phone down, he heard Dyer's voice say, "I still think about her."

Harris tried the front door of Sienna's place. It was locked. Behind the house, there was a shed with cast-iron bars on the windows, a padlock on the door. He stood in the rain and looked inside with a flashlight. An office. Filing cabinets. A map over the desk. Turnell Island.

Something moved in fast from one side. A blow landed and Harris fell into the grass and water. Chaos and alcohol raged through him. He slumped over. As his eyes began to shutter, he heard a voice say, "Bring him up."

A slap snapped him out of it. Harris could only see through one eye. He couldn't move. They had him in a chair, his left hand cuffed to a railing. He looked around: he was on the deck of the house overlooking the shed. Without notice, he vomited onto the timber.

A second slap came.

"Oh no, Dee Dee, you keep slapping him, he'll just keep sicking up all over the place. Are you an idiot? No. Just leave him be a moment."

Harris brought his head up. He felt drool and blood slide out of his mouth and over his chin.

The Italian from the beach, Al Sienna. He stood over him. Behind him, a monstrously tall man in a black tracksuit kept watch.

"Here," said Sienna, handing him a packet of frozen peas, "for your head."

Harris took it. "You remember me?"

"I know who you are, Detective Harris. Bit late for a visit though, yes?"

Harris didn't know what to say.

Al hunched down, looked him in the eye. "I hear you've been around though, bothering the Spinanes, checking files. You don't call me, though. Instead you come here at night, scare my wife, force Dee Dee here to raise his hand to you. What is this all in aid of, huh?"

"I'm looking for David Thompson."

"This is a not so good person to be looking for," said Sienna.

A door opened behind them. They both turned.

A woman's voice said, "Alessio?"

Sienna went to her and spoke in fast Italian. She was ancient. Al turned to Dee Dee and said something. The giant uncuffed him, picked him up under the shoulders.

"Can you walk?" said the giant.

Harris nodded.

The door closed.

Harris and the giant took the stairs and walked across to the shed. As the giant recuffed him to an office chair, he watched Sienna come over holding an umbrella. As soon as he was inside, he grabbed Harris by the hair and yanked his head back. "You idiot. You wake my mother as well."

He let Harris go and settled himself.

"Maybe it's time we had a little drink," he said.

The Italian poured wine into two coffee mugs. Harris noticed his service revolver sticking out of the waistband of the man's pajamas.

Sienna handed over the wine.

Harris looked in the mug. "I don't really…"

"It must be the only thing you don't drink. You smell like shit. Take it, it'll do you the world of good."

Harris took a small sip. It tasted okay.

"Good, good. Now, I can not help you with this

David Thompson business," said Sienna. "He's dead." He spat on the floor between them. "But maybe I can help you with something else. And you can help me, yes? We know each other, don't we? Yes we do, I think."

Sienna waved to a filing cabinet, and Dee Dee opened it and retrieved a file. Al sorted through it until he found what he was looking for. He threw the rest on the desk. He then took a chair and brought it close to Harris, opening the pages for him.

It was a set of photographs.

"Let me see," said Sienna and he began to turn them over, one by one.

Harris and the licensing boys coming out of the Palm Relaxo.

Harris and Caller standing on the beach, around the beach fire, with three prostitutes.

Harris asleep on the sand. There was just enough sun to make out the half-naked woman lying beside him. She smiled up at the camera. They had his cock out. The girl's hand offering it up to the lens.

"You remember some of this? Yes?" said Sienna. "I take no joy in showing you these things. I think these memories, happy memories I think, they should stay just between friends, yes?"

Harris took another mouthful of wine.

"And of course, you have also been busy up here, haven't you, Detective."

Sienna took a yellow envelope from the file and opened it.

More photos, originals.

Sarah Hannon kissing him on the doorstep of the motel.

Hannon in her bra by the window, his arms around her.

Hannon kneeling over him on the bed.

The two of them naked.

Harris leaned in and said, "How did you—"

"Oh?" said Sienna. "I have your attention now? Good. I know who this is. I've been here long enough to know. Dee Dee here even went to the same school as the two of you, a couple of years behind weren't you, Dee Dee?"

The giant nodded.

Harris felt the room constrict around him.

"You've been a naughty boy, Detective Harris. But this is okay, I think. I don't approve but we can move past this. I spend my whole life around men who take what they shouldn't."

"Just leave my sister out of this," said Harris.

Harris felt himself starting to cry.

"I remember Lachlan too," said Sienna. "He did a bit of work for my brother Sal, back in the day. See, we both have idiot brothers, brothers who don't know how to behave in the world. Brothers who make trouble. These brothers are everywhere. This David Thompson, Sal, your brother. This is just life, yes?"

"No," said Harris. It came out weak.

"This is okay," said Sienna, patting his shoulder. "This is okay."

They all waited in the room until the moment started to pass. Al Sienna put his feet up on the desk and pointed at the map of Turnell Island. "How would you like a holiday house overlooking the ocean?" he said. "This is… This here is a place where no one asks too many questions. You probably belong in a nice place like this, Detective Harris. How about you and I work together? Yes?"

They turned him loose as the sun rose. Al Sienna gave him a Turnell Island prospectus, a bag of lemons, and his empty service revolver. Harris looked at the glossy brochure in the car while waiting for the lights to change. They could have killed him. But all he had to do was stop poking around and return a favor. Whatever the case, they knew he was coming now. It sounded like they always knew he might be. There was no backing out.

Harris let himself doze for an hour before popping another dexy. He pinned parts of the Turnell Island prospectus to the motel room wall, on the Laura Spinane chart. The island sat out at the end of a branch that linked David and Laura to the Sienna brothers.

He picked up the phone and dialed.

Ann Spinane picked up.

"How did Laura end up in a brothel? Weren't you supposed to be looking after her?"

"Who is this?" said Spinane.

"Why didn't you do something?" He heard himself screaming.

The line went dead.

Harris went back to the charts.

He looked at the LACHLAN one.

Finished.

He looked at LAURA.

Unfinished.

Harris stood between them and knew that this was all just repetition. No chaos. No disorder. Violence perpetrated by two angry brothers, in two different stories.

He let himself feel it.

The two charts started to wind together. White and black, then and now. They circled one another with a symmetry that felt unnatural but locked tight. Only one destination now. It made sense. Harris stared into the space in between the two charts and saw the spiral's end.

Harris paid the motel owner to keep the room, no cleaners.

He booked a flight to Brisbane, one way.

As he packed, Sarah Hannon came to the door. He had it open.

"On the run again, I see."

He pointed at the LACHLAN chart. "I'm done with that. When it's over, bring the detectives here."

Hannon's face dropped. She came in and looked. Her lipstick writing sat at one end, with the photos, clippings, dates and victims trailing off. Harris had pasted two pages of handwritten text at the end.

"My confession," he said. "I left you out of it."

"I can't bring people to this," she said.

He grabbed her and screamed, "It all finishes here."

She pushed back, catching him in the face with a short punch. Harris let himself sway. When the wall caught him, he slid down and sat. Hannon stood over him, rubbing her knuckles. He looked up at her and she kicked him. In a rage, she started beating her hands against the wall, tearing at the chart. Harris stopped her. He held her arms. After she stopped struggling, he kissed her and she kissed him back. She pulled him back against the chart, and as he unbuttoned her uniform they seemed to evaporate into the history of it.

THE HISTORY OF IT

THEY HAD TWO FATHERS: Lachlan, the oldest brother who acted like a father and Sammy, the man who made them but seemed to forget it while he sat there, year after year, drinking himself stupid. Their mother was long gone, not much more than a ghost in their memory. "You didn't miss much," said Lachlan. Their father never spoke her name: Margaret Hannon.

Jim Harris couldn't pinpoint when the degradation started. He knew enough about abuse and horror to realize that it went way back. It didn't just start — it felt as if it did, as if one day after school, he found his brother Lachlan and sister Sarah in the bathroom — but it was hardwired into them all from the beginning. It was part of them, part of Lachlan, and Lachlan was everything: the head of the family, the local sporting hero, the leader.

Lachlan was all ideas.

Lachlan only looked at Sarah. He knew it was wrong.

He made Harris act.

When Harris and Sarah didn't do as they were told, Lachlan had Sammy do the only parenting Sammy was good for, a beating. And it went on for years.

The only peace came with the away games. Lachlan travelled far and wide with the league team. Some of those dates added up now. The pattern charted. There were broken children everywhere Lachlan went.

For Sarah and Harris, the chasm faded shut during the long slow summer of 1973. Harris could finally throw a punch in '73. It took a while but eventually even Lachlan could see the end of it. Lachlan moved out, went to Darwin, and became a bouncer in a nightclub. He raged and evolved. They heard the stories. The police visited, every now and then.

At sixteen, Harris went to Brisbane.

At nineteen, he'd landed in the police academy.

Sarah struggled through the beginnings of high school.

Sammy stayed the same.

Cairns as a war-zone.

Cairns as a discrete compartment, locked away.

At sixteen, Sarah came to Brisbane to visit.

"I missed you," she said.

Harris felt it too.

They spent a weekend in the darkness, entirely of their own accord. After that, Harris would think of his brother at the firing range. He'd dream of the bullets opening Lachlan up, spilling every secret out of him. He started to fantasize.

* * *

The year of his second posting, Harris got the call he now thought of as a trigger. The start of the end.

Sarah: "He's back. He's been coming round. He stands outside the house."

Lachlan.

The calls kept coming:

"He's been inside."

"He's been talking to Dad on the phone."

"I'm scared."

Whatever drove Lachlan to do the things he did, it found full expression in Darwin. He came back to Cairns as a more violent man, addicted to speed and blood and fear.

He was back for Sarah.

One day in autumn, Lachlan made his move. He came in during the night. Tied Sarah and Sammy up in the living room and paced around with a hunting knife. He ranted so loud the police came.

Lachlan untied them as the sirens arrived. When the police walked in, Sammy didn't say a word. Sarah stood there in her piss-soaked nightie and stared. They put Lachlan in the drunk tank. He was out the next day.

Sarah saved her money.

She came back to Brisbane.

She made him promise. She made him commit:

Lachlan had to go.

Harris bought an unassigned seat on the train and went back to Cairns. He went to the house and stayed the night. Sammy didn't like it but he kept his mouth shut.

The three of them, the Harris family, waited together for a week.

Eventually he called.

Harris answered, "I'm back for a while. You better come round and sort this out."

Lachlan had no idea. When he arrived, Harris could see that there wasn't much of him left. His eyes were blank. He was a mad dog, smelled like a street crazy, his hair knotted around his shoulders.

As soon as Sarah closed the front door behind him, Harris laid him out with a king hit, cuffed him, gagged him, and rolled him over. They put him in the cardboard box the laundry machine came in and put him in the back of his own panel van. Harris threw an old carpet over him and placed the shovel and the bag of lime in beside. He turned the radio on. As they drove out of town, it was like he wasn't even there.

Out in the night, deep into bush land, they let him out. He was in shock but it didn't matter. He was still Lachlan. He stood there, in the glare of the van spotlights and ranted. He made no real sense. He had no handle on the situation. When he saw the gun, he said, "What, Jim? Are you going to shoot me now?"

The first bullet caught him just below the nose, pushing most of his brains out through the back of his head. He stood for a while like that. Harris fired again. He fell. They buried him right there, after Sarah smashed his corpse to pieces with the shovel.

DAY 2:
WEDNESDAY, JANUARY 22, 1986

THE PLANE LANDED IN Brisbane at midday. He took a cab to a cheap hotel in the Valley. While he waited, Harris cleaned his gun and plotted.

Matt came at four. He had the files.

The kid looked like hell. He had a bottle of scotch in his hand and half a load on from lunch. He wasn't going to last. Harris made coffee.

"What's the plan?" said Dyer.

"I'm going to take the bull by the horns. You're going to stay out the way. At the end of this, someone's going to get a medal. It may as well be you."

"No. No, I—"

"I made a promise to your dad. This—" Harris picked up the file, "—is enough. It's more than enough to put you right in the middle of it. But tonight, tomorrow, this is all going to hell and, if you want to get square, this is your part. You don't want to ride along. Trust me."

"I'm coming," said Dyer.

Harris grabbed the kid by the collar and pushed him towards a mirror in the hallway. He lifted his head with rough force and said, "Look at yourself. You're good to no one," and that was the end of it.

Dyer went out to drink it off.

Harris's head and shoulder pounded from Sienna's beating. He washed down two pills with aspirin.

He laid files and ran the dates.

He got down to it:

They were all out in Gatton the night Laura Spinane died. Except Blintiff. Gatton was an hour out of town. It wouldn't take much to come back in. Harris rang the Brisbane CIB exchange and got put through to Danny O'Shea. O'Shea was still the same shithead but they'd promoted him after the Gatton thing. O'Shea was climbing the pole.

"I need help," he said.

"Oh really? Detective Jim Harris," said O'Shea. "I thought ya worked for the water police or some shite up north. Ya still with us? There ya go. Shows how much I know."

"I'm running a lead," said Harris.

"Missing dog? Someone lose their wallet at the pub?"

"Dead girl. The whodunnit from '85. I'm not sure it came together quite like how Richo wrote it up back then. Ringing any bells?"

"Fooking Richo. I've just cleaned up another mess of his. I'm trying to fire that cunt but the union won't give me an inch on it."

Harris almost laughed. "Good luck with that."

"What has Richo cocked up now? Tell me."

"We had your Gatton guy down for the Spinane thing. The write-up had him coming in from Gatton, bumping off Laura, and then running back out there to get himself shot."

"Yeah, seems plausible," said O'Shea, with a sigh.

"I want to know what the licensing boys were doing out there?"

"They were assisting with an official police investigation, and getting overtime. Half the bloody office scored a drink off that thing."

"What about Caller?"

"Barry? He was in and out."

"Can you check your diary?"

Harris could hear O'Shea moving around, a swivel of his office chair. Harris remembered the office. O'Shea was checking out who was in earshot.

"You there?" said Harris.

"Barry didn't do a fooking thing in Gatton. I didn't see him," said O'Shea, before hanging up.

Harris looked at his notes and thought about the LAURA chart in Cairns. He sorted information. He went straight to the piece that hurt the most.

The gray utility.

Birdy. The bed.

"You remember the car at all?"

"It was a ute."

"What color?"

"Dark, gray."

He pushed it back down.

This wasn't for her. This was for all of them.

* * *

He opened the files Dyer brought him. He spread everything out on the floor and looked. The whole mess. The licensing boys were everywhere in it. They were tied up with the whole box and dice.

Harris collated their recent arrests. They were clamping down. Brisbane was on the cusp of something new, and it looked like Caller and his gang were making show. In the last three months they'd raided brothels, arrested bludgers, and tagged along on a casino raid. On paper, they were reforming Brisbane.

They needed to.

Harris went further back.

The top brass and a corruption task force made a pass at them last year. They were put under investigation for illegally obtained income. There were asset tests. Suspected links to organized crime. The lot.

And then nothing.

Inconclusive evidence. Signed and dated August 1985, by none other than the Inspector, the Old Bloke himself, up to his guts in it as well.

Not a whisper since.

Harris turned it over.

The writing was on the wall for these blokes: they were cleaning up the loose ends now. They were cashing out.

Harris suspected he knew where the money was headed: up north, to the Siennas, to this Turnell Island caper.

He thought about a drink.

He popped a pill out of the foil but left it on the bench.

Two days without sleep.

He hit the living room couch like a lead balloon.

In his dreams, Birdy danced a slow motion dance around a bonfire while Harris, covered in blood, killed them all one at a time.

DAY 3:
THURSDAY, JANUARY 23, 1986

IN THE MORNING, HE told Dyer to go get his father and get out of town. "Tell them whatever you need to," he said. "Just never admit I was here. I'll send my notes. You can do the rest, when I'm done."

"You going to be okay?" said Dyer.

"I'm going to bow out. This is my last hurrah."

Harris went to the traffic office and had showed his ID to the clerk before they had the shutter all the way up. He pulled every car record for everyone in licensing and their immediate families.

It was a wasted effort. The damned thing was right there on the first page: a grey tray back utility registered to Barry Reginald Caller. His off-duty car.

Harris let a fast vision of Birdy pass.

He went to a pay phone and called the Brisbane office.

Jangles answered.

"Sorry, Sergeant Caller is off today, can I—"

"Wrong number," said Harris.

He called Roy Dyer's place. He wasn't happy. "What the bloody hell are you doing back here, Jim?"

"Put Matt on."

They talked. Matt rang off and called back a few minutes later. "Yeah mate, Caller's off sick. Hasn't been in all week. And you're not going to like this."

"What is it?"

"Blintiff too."

He rented a car and drove out to The Gap, where Caller lived. Harris sat on the house for hours. Caller had a family, a wife, children, and January was the school holidays. Harris brooded. The Caller house was not the result of a policeman's salary. It was a two-story timber place, high ceilings, a new roof, a long enclosed verandah along the front. And it was for sale, a sign on the lawn.

Mid-morning, a slim blonde woman came down the front stairs. She looked good, about fifteen years younger than Caller. The woman had two young girls with her. She loaded them into a bronze Fairlane and backed out. With the car idling in the drive, she opened a second garage door and dragged the bins out onto the curb. When she did that, Harris took a long look at her and the grey ute parked inside the house.

Nothing about it felt good.

He waited five minutes and went over. The day was bright hot and there was no cover. He opened the screen, unholstered his gun, and knocked. Slow footsteps slumped their way up to the door and it opened.

Caller in a green bathrobe, looking like death warmed up. "What did you—"

He took one look at Harris and ran. Harris caught him in the hallway and put him down with a single jab. He dragged the man along the polished timber to the kitchen and dumped him.

Caller groaned and spat.

Harris took a glass from the sink and filled it. He popped a dexy.

"How you feeling, Barry?"

Caller crawled over to a wall and sat up against it, wincing the whole time.

"What do you want, Harris?"

Harris had electrical tape, a box cutter, and a gun but he hadn't really thought it through. He looked around. The house had heavy exposed beams in the ceiling. He went to Caller and stretched out the tape. "I like this get-up, Barry," he said.

Caller gurgled and wheezed. Getting him bound and strung up was no easy task. He was a mess. He didn't seem to see it coming but Harris had to hit him another couple of times to get it done. Caller now stood in the center of his own kitchen, on a chair, with his head in a noose. He didn't have enough height to be comfortable; the belt of his bathrobe bit into his neck. He stayed up on his toes, swiveling like a lure.

"Relax, idiot," said Harris. "You keep moving around, you're going to die."

"Please," said Caller.

Harris held up a photo of Laura Spinane and David Thompson. "The girl, that body I picked up last year and you pissed away? Remember her? Last seen getting into a grey ute, just like yours. Her brother, your protégé, disappears around the same time, in Cairns."

Harris took out his notepad, turned back to February '85.

"She was looking for him. She *liked* cops, apparently."

"Please, please."

"What happened to her?"

"No, no, please," said Caller.

Harris put his hand on the chair holding Caller in place, and he started to panic. "Thompson," said Caller. "Thompson killed—"

"Nope. Thompson saved his sister. So, okay then, what really happened to Thompson?"

"Gone," said Caller.

"Gone where?"

He shook his head and closed his eyes. Tears streamed down his face.

"Barry, you look like shit. You've been sick, I hear."

Caller kept on gasping.

"You know you're dying, right?" said Harris. "Your wife is probably on her way out too. And Jesus, who knows, maybe your kids have it too, I'm no doctor. It's nasty shit, the bug you've got. I think I know where you caught it."

The right angle. His eyes opened. Wrath.

Harris stared back. "What are they going to do when you're in the ground, dickhead?"

"She fucking killed me," said Caller. "She killed all of us, right when—"

"Why would she do a thing like that, Barry?"

He shook his head, almost smiled. "So close."

"Tell me," said Harris.

He was done. "Thompson had to go. He was making waves. He bloody went and topped Sienna's brother a couple of nights after that thing in Cairns. We had everything in with them. He nearly fucked the whole thing up."

"And his sister?"

"Blintiff got hammered and bragged about it, told Spiny we offed a Cairns bloke once when he found out she was from up there. We didn't know who she was. Or why she was putting it around for free."

Harris put his foot on the chair, applied a little pressure.

"How'd you put it together?"

"We didn't. Al Sienna was in town. He was looking for the girl. She was a loose end. He told me about what she had. His brother bloody gave it to her. She was after us from the moment she landed."

"For her brother?"

"Christ." Caller started praying, "Our Father, who art in heaven."

Harris applied more pressure.

"Hallowed be Thy name."

The chair swung a little. He leaned forward.

"Thy kingdom come…"

The survival instinct started to kick in.

"…will be done…I…I just picked her up."

Caller stared at the ceiling. The sun rained in through the back windows.

"Who then?"

They both knew.

"Blintiff," he said. "He's…"

"Yeah, we'll see," said Harris and kicked the chair out.

With his last breaths, Caller said, "He's mine, he's mine, he was my own..."

It made no sense to Harris. He held the man still as he rattled around on the line. Shit and spit filed out of him. When it was over, Harris washed his hands in the sink and regretted it. Killing Caller was a kindness he didn't deserve.

Caller had an office in the garage and Harris found what he needed. The nerve of the man was astounding. He had a handwritten ledger in a locked drawer. The key under a coffee mug on the table above. There were files as well. Harris took the lot. He started to wipe the place down until he remembered that it didn't matter.

Blintiff lived in a low-set bungalow in Coorparoo. Harris checked a window and moved down the side. Out the back, the building's windows had been taped over with plastic sheeting. The place smelled like fresh paint. Blintiff was renovating.

Harris knocked on the rear door.

Nothing.

He kicked it in.

The house was borderline empty. Blintiff lived lean. He had a plastic outdoor setting in the living room, a single bed in one of the rooms. That was it. The oven was disconnected. Blintiff had a camp cooker on the kitchen bench. Harris recognized the vibe. No excess material. No unnecessary detail. No distraction. No future.

The only decoration was a Polaroid photograph stuck to the door of one of the rooms. That room was padlocked from the outside. The photo showed Blintiff as a young kid, standing next to what looked like his old man in military fatigues. Harris pulled the Polaroid down and shuddered. In neat cursive pencil, someone had captioned the back: Barracks, Coopers Plains, 1952.

The padlock was heavy. Harris searched the kitchen drawers for a key and turned up a screwdriver instead. He unwound each screw in the staple. As the last of five dropped to the floor, Harris gently pushed the door open.

The room was empty.

Plastic sheeting covered the windows and floor.

The room smelled like bleach and something familiar.

Harris stepped in, the plastic flooring greasy underfoot.

He looked closer.

Every inch of the room, from baseboard to ceiling, was wallpapered in pornography. The flesh tones of thousands of women, carefully cut from magazines and pasted into place. Harris took in hardcore details. Yawning orifices. Cocks like serpents. Mouths and assholes stretched to breaking point.

The careful arrangement spelled closeted insanity.

Harris felt his stomach rise.

He lifted his foot and peered down at the ground.

Semen. It was everywhere.

Harris ran.

Harris spent the afternoon trying to run him down. By dusk, the Dyers had decamped to Toowoomba and he had Matt call around from up there. Blintiff wasn't in the pubs. He wasn't in the office. He wasn't out on the street.

Harris stared at himself in the rearview mirror.

"Think," he said to himself. He needed the charts.

He went back to the motel and opened Caller's ledger. He spread the dead man's files over the table. Matt Dyer called back just after eight. No sign of Blintiff but the word was out, "They found Caller. They know someone was there when he necked himself. Jangles is looking for you."

Harris took the paperwork and drove.

He rented a room out near the airport. He kept working.

He shotgunned dexies and read through the night.

He photographed the books with a camera.

As the sun came up, he figured he had one play left, and it was a long-odds bet.

DAY 4:
FRIDAY, JANUARY 24, 1986

THE SUMMER NIGHTS BROTHEL did a roaring dawn trade. Every loser ended up there. As he waited at the door, Harris figured he looked like any other punter. Worse, probably. A man Harris didn't recognize let him in. He should have known.

As soon as the door closed, Roberto Agrioli stepped in behind and laid the first punch, a blinding uppercut to his side. Roberto's second punch landed right where Harris was already sore. He crumpled like a paper bag. Another man rushed in and helped Roberto, the two of them working him over quickly, right there in the pink reception room. When they were done, Roberto hoisted Harris up and dumped him out a side door.

"Wait, wait," said Harris.

Roberto came back and clocked him in the stomach, pushing all the air out of him.

Harris covered his head.

"No," he gasped. They'd rushed into this. Harris still had his revolver. He crawled up and dragged the gun out.

Roberto froze.

Harris felt close to unconsciousness. He put the gun to his own temple and stared Roberto down. "Wait," he said again. "If I pull the trigger, you go back to the can, no question." He pointed the gun at Roberto. "Or maybe I shoot you, then I shoot myself?"

Roberto looked like he was going to have a seizure.

"I want to talk to the boss," said Harris. "That's what I'm here for. I'm not here for you."

"What?"

"I want a sit down. Then you and I can talk some more if you like."

Roberto went for it. No sane person, especially a Brisbane copper, would ask for this unless it was important. People who sat down with the Agrioli's upper management often didn't get up again. So Roberto helped Harris inside, plonked him down at a table by a phone. Joe Agrioli was on the line, Roberto's brother. Joe was not the top of the chain but close enough. Joe listened to the pitch and said:

"I'm coming round. Put Robbie back on."

For an hour Roberto and Harris waited in the small kitchen above the brothel; Harris caked in dried blood, slipping in and out of consciousness in his chair, the gun still in his hand. Roberto stood by the door, staring into space, spooked.

When Joe arrived, he ignored the gun. He sat at the table and said, "This had better be good, or you'll be waking up in the river."

Harris opened his coat and took out a folded piece of paper. "The licensing boys are cashing out," he said.

"Tell me something I don't know."

Harris unfolded the slip and turned it around for him. "They're buying an island with a Cairns outfit. This is one page of where the money's going. But I have the whole lot. Have a look at some of the names here."

Agrioli read a page from Caller's ledger.

They were all there:

The Sienna family.

Councilors.

State pollies.

Department heads.

Bank CEOs.

Joe Agrioli didn't see it.

Roberto clenched and unclenched his fists in the background.

"Those people can get anything done in this state," said Harris.

"So?"

"There's a long list of suppliers in the rest of it. They've got architects and planners, blokes who specialize in casinos, hotels, tourism. They've got international money coming in from all over. They've got biker money, Asian money, some crew from the Netherlands. Caller and his boys are only the tip of it."

Agrioli sat back. He gently touched the line of his scalp.

Harris went for it: "My guess is, they're closing down Brisbane. And they're opening up this Turnell Island caper instead. You look at the stuff I have, you can see it plain as day. This is going to be Amsterdam off the coast of Rocky and I don't see you guys anywhere near it. They're cutting you out. Caller and a bunch of Brisbane coppers are using your money, a decade of graft that *you* handed over, to fund their buy-in. They're going to put you out of business with it."

"From what I hear, Caller isn't buying into anything," said Agrioli. He lit a cigarette and passed the pack to Harris. "What do you want for this? Money?"

"I want Blintiff. I can't find him."

Agrioli smiled. He turned to Roberto.

Roberto shrugged.

"He's gone," Joe Agrioli said.

"Where?"

"Up north, we hear…to kill you."

"So what now, fuckhead?" said Roberto.

"I'll give you everything I've got on them but I want someone looked after. And I want a chartered plane and your word that certain people get left out of the blood-letting. And I need some more pills, something to keep me moving."

Joe nodded. He held out his hand.

There was blood dripping from Harris's fingers. "You don't want to shake on this," he said. "But it's a deal. And you," he turned to Roberto, "you might want to go to the doctor. You never know what you might catch off another bloke in an alleyway in this neck of the woods."

The plane was a single-engine Cessna and it pitched around like a ping pong ball in the wind. Harris tried to sleep. The pilot didn't want to know any of it. He kept his eyes on the sky ahead.

As soon as they landed, Harris went to the bathroom and puked. He had a bag of speed. The Agriolis didn't do prescription stuff. Harris snorted a big fat line in the airfield restroom and it roared through him like lightning.

As he walked out into the early morning humidity, Harris felt separated from himself. His body ached. He had a slight limp and he could feel himself bleeding into the gauze.

He knew it then. There'd only be a couple of hours left.

Day Four.

So this was where it would end.

Fucking Cairns.

There was nowhere to hide. Everyone knew where Harris was, where he lived, where to find him. Harris got out of the cab a block out from the motel. There was a pub on the corner and he went in and called the motel owner. The owner hadn't seen anyone matching Blintiff's description but that didn't mean much. "People come and go round here, mate. I don't get paid to mess about with—"

"I want the room across from mine," said Harris. "I have a friend coming to stay. Is it available?"

The clerk checked.

"The one just up from it is."

"I'll pay you tomorrow. Go and open it up. Put the keys on the dresser."

Harris went to the bar. He ordered a whisky and put it down in one go.

So much for his last drink.

He went back to the phone and called Sarah Hannon.

No answer.

He tried the station house.

"Harris, right," said the desk sergeant. "There was a bloke in from Brisbane looking for you. Drove up last night. And you've got, ya know, a few messages here. Nothing pressing."

"Where is this bloke?"

"Just around. He said he'd call back every couple of hours."

Harris looked around the pub and thought it out.

"Tell him I was in Brisbane on business but I'm back now."

"Will do, mate."

"Is Constable Hannon around?"

"Nah," he said. "She's out on patrol."

Harris left a message for Sam Peters. He asked him to come visit the motel tomorrow morning. It wasn't fair but it was the best way he could think up.

He rang Matt Dyer and said goodbye.

"My case notes and a roll of film are in the mail," said Harris. "You're going to need them."

Dyer had a strange read on it. He didn't ask. Almost out of politeness he said, "What are you going to do now? You sound like you're back home?"

"I am," said Harris.

The motel was deserted. There was no sign of Blintiff's car. Not much chance of him hiding out on the grounds either. He didn't figure Blintiff for a guy who'd spend the day standing in the downstairs laundry waiting. He'd come after dark.

Harris set himself up in the room across the courtyard. The motel arced around like a horseshoe, a thin terrace on the second level. From his new room, Harris had a good line of sight. He put the TV on in his old room. Light flickered behind the curtain. The trap was set and the speed kept him diamond sharp.

It was everything he could think to do yet as he sat there waiting, he found a new pocket of fear in himself. The pain worried him. The big nothing scared him. Getting it right would be no easy task. Harris wanted it to be over, and the last gasp of his life seemed like a long list of smaller items to attend to, none of them good.

He paced.

He called the hospital. A nurse checked on his blood work.

Seconds passed like hours.

"You there?" said the nurse.

"Yeah, I'm here," he said.

"Okay, Mr. Harris. Some of this doesn't look so good. You need to come and see us."

Harris went to put the phone down but didn't. Instead, he sat there with the receiver in his hands and stared at it.

"Mr. Harris?"

He didn't move.

"Mr. Harris?"

"I'm here," he said. "I can't come in."

"You're in the early stages of liver disease. If you were ten years older, you'd be dead. You need treatment. And there's a few other things going on here that I don't like the look of. You need to make a major lifestyle change, Mr. Harris. Immediately."

"What about the AIDS?"

"No, that side of things looks okay. Were you at risk?"

"I was," he said.

He put the phone down and breathed out. His hands started to shake. The relief felt exactly like torment. He let himself lay back on the bed and the room spun, as if sucked up into an invisible drain hole above.

They came a little before midnight. Blintiff was making no pretense to negotiation. He carried a shotgun by his leg and had a broad, tall man walking with him. As they came across the road, Harris recognized the other one: Dee Dee, the giant.

They made their way up the stairs to the second tier, level with him. Harris gently nudged the door open. He watched through the crack. Blintiff worked the lock with a pick. Dee Dee stood watch.

They were exposed.

In one fluid movement, Harris came out the door and fired.

The first shot missed completely. Glass shattered.

He squeezed the trigger again.

Dee Dee flew back.

Harris tracked over to Blintiff and fired. The man screamed and disappeared into the room. Harris ran the terrace, gun trained on the door.

Shots cracked in the night. His room lit with each one. The rail by Harris pinged and sparked. Glass and debris flew around him. Something caught the edge of his waist and tripped him. He scrambled up and kept running. He popped shots in through the doorway. As he came up on the mouth of the room he fell out of range and Blintiff quit firing.

Terrified, Harris reached into his jacket pocket and pushed fresh bullets into his gun. He dropped a handful and in slow-motion horror, watched them roll over the edge of the terrace.

Harris counted to four and took a look inside.

Blintiff was sitting up in the bed. No shotgun.

Another shot sounded. The door frame exploded.

"You dead yet?" Harris shouted.

More shots came, one ripped a hole in the plasterboard beside him. Dust sprayed.

Harris panicked. He went for it. Something heavy hit him. Blintiff crawled across the bed in the low light and Harris followed him with the gun, pulling on the trigger. Blood sprayed out of Blintiff's body and smoke filled the room. As Harris got within a foot of him, Blintiff stopped moving.

Harris stood there and breathed.

He ran a hand over his chest, lifted the hand.

Blood.

He took a quick glance down: a light wound on his side. Harris scanned the floor. A service revolver sat by the door. Blintiff had gotten desperate: he'd thrown his empty gun at him as he came in.

Harris checked on Dee Dee. The big man's body was slumped into the wall outside, as if he sat backwards, the paintwork beside him sprayed dark. He wasn't getting up. He wasn't doing anything again.

Harris went back inside and hit the light switch. He took in the whole scene. Shell casings, splintered timber. The ripped mattress. Torn walls. The charts, Laura and Lachlan's legacies, covered in gore. More gore. Harris went to the wall above the bed and looked at a photo of his family. He wiped blood from the face of his sister and left the rest of them veiled. He looked again at the whole thing and decided it was enough.

Someone would work the rest out.

Only one thing left.

But not here.

Harris went to his bathroom and washed his hands. He took another bump of speed and choked down another crying jag. The drug did its job. The shock pushed him back outside.

He was about to leave when he heard Blintiff mumbling. He'd moved a little. Harris went to him and squatted down beside the bed. Blintiff turned his head and spat out a ropey mess of blood and saliva. The man's eyes showed raw terror.

"No," said Blintiff.

Harris sighed.

He stood up and fired again.

As the sirens sounded in the distance, Harris walked through the streets of Cairns to the ocean. He could feel eyes on him — house lights coming on — but no one stepped out. He limped along, gun in hand, alone.

On the beach he peeled off his jacket and walked down to the water, stepping in up to his knees. He watched the dark sea roll around until the lights flashed behind.

"Jim!"

He knew the voice.

Sam Peters and Sarah Hannon stood on the shoreline half in silhouette, their guns and flashlights drawn.

Peters was out front. "You gotta put that gun down, Jim."

He stared at them.

Nothing came to mind.

"What now?" said Sarah.

Peters looked confused.

Harris put the gun to his head.

"No, Jim, stop," said Sam. He treaded into the water.

"Go on, then," said Hannon.

Waves broke behind him. Foam came up around his legs.

Peters was close.

"See you soon," she said.

Harris pulled on the trigger.

Click.

Click.

Click.

Cl—

EPILOGUE
TUNNEL ISLAND
2003

He stared into her eyes and looked at her hair and it was all still in there.

"Let's go into the other room," said Harris.

He watched the brunette put on the gear, the latex cat suit, the heels.

She clapped her hands when she was done.

They never found David Thompson's body. Detective Hearst, the one they called Jangles, was the only one left who might have known, and he didn't live long enough to tell anyone. They found him in his car, half his head missing.

He was the only cop the Agrioli family took care of that way. That was the warning for every dirty cop who went it alone.

They really cleaned house.

The warning they sent the other families was worse. The force of it, and the speed, shocked the whole country. Within a fortnight of the motel shoot-out, they'd waged war.

* * *

The brunette cuffed Harris and took him through to the other room. It was dark, lit by two spotlights. She kissed him, ran a hand over his crotch. She smelled like apples.

"You're a piece of garbage, Jim Harris," she said.

He nodded.

"Put your hands up, do it now."

She fastened the cuffs to a steel loop in the ceiling.

While he watched, she went over to a work bench they had in there. It was covered in a soft black material. She peeled it back and the whips sat in a neat orderly line.

"What should we do here?" she said, "What to do? So many options."

She picked up a timber paddle.

"I don't think you deserve this," she said. "I only use this on people who I can help."

Harris stared at her.

"This," she said, picking up a black riding crop.

She came to him and unbuckled the pants of his pretend police uniform. They fell. She squatted down and roughly dragged down his underwear. "This," she said, "is disgusting. I should cut this off and feed it to you."

Harris nodded.

"It's what I deserve," he said.

She walked around and got into position.

The Agrioli family killed everyone.

The Sienna house was a bloodbath. They did the lot. Laid Al Sienna, his wife and his mother out on the back lawn like a cat would with dead birds. In fact, they even killed the family cat and put it down there with them. A local alderman in Rockhampton met a similar fate. They dumped him in a fountain, alongside his own arms. And circling all that obvious stuff were more bodies that looked suspicious. There were overdoses and suicides and emergency overseas trips. An architect with no interest in fishing suddenly had a boating accident. The blood ran free. And the message came through loud and clear: Turnell Island now belonged to the Agriolis.

Matt Dyer rode it all the way to the top. They tasked him with overseeing the whole mess and he did what he could, with what he had, to keep things orderly.

He had a few wins.

The Old Bloke, the Inspector, stood down.

Support flowed in. The violence scared everyone.

One of the weirder loose ends was Salvatore Sienna. They found him in a shallow grave down the back of the Spinane family property in Cairns. An anonymous tip-off. And as they dug up the body and filed it as a cold case, no one realized that he was the idiot that sunk the whole caper. Laura Spinane's pimp, her boyfriend, her infector. The man who brought the rage out of David Thompson and knocked the future of Turnell Island out of line, taking the retirement plans of corrupt cops and gangsters with it.

The first lash from the whip caught Harris across the thighs. The pain rippled through him.

Every thought of David Thompson vanished.

His mind buzzed.

Harris got off. Barry Caller's suicide was a closed book. Blintiff and Dee Dee went down the chute unsolved, pegged as "gangland activity." No charges were laid.

Instead, the department quietly put him out to pasture. They put him in a hospital. A year of white walls and bad food. Twelve months of bad conversation and counseling. When that was done, they parked him in AA.

At the tail end of the twelve steps, Harris knew he was broken for good. He didn't want a damned thing, especially forgiveness. While everyone else daydreamed of a new drug or a new fuck or just-one-more-drink, Harris sat there on his folding chair and felt nothing.

By the time he was back out in the world, it was a changed landscape. The Fitzgerald Inquiry rolled through Brisbane after Dyer's task force and it was like a summer plague to police corruption. It ate all the crops, all the spoils. The Queensland Police were never the same. Even Dyer said it was like working in a community center compared to what it once was. Harris only saw him once or twice. His career was no triumph. That success never righted him.

And nothing really changed. While the political rebuilding hosed Brisbane clean, Turnell Island set down its roots and they were worse than anything that came before it. The illegal casinos went legit over there. The brothels diversified. Drugs, money, guns, vice, it all went offshore. A decade in, the place was so flush with cash they built that tunnel down under the bay so the tourists could drive there. It worked. It was a glorified sewer pipe. And all of the state's garbage spewed out of it. The locals started calling it Tunnel Island. The name stuck.

For his sins, the Agriolis gave him the same deal Al Sienna offered: an apartment on the island. The department left him on the books. The nudge was gentle but it came from all sides. Everyone wanted him out-of-sight and Turnell was the best option. His posting there was cheaper and quieter than firing him, and they didn't fire people who knew what he knew.

Twenty years later, he found it tolerable.

Harris found himself a special kind of brothel, one that worked with pain more than pleasure. He paid for his punishment by the hour.

The brunette teased with the whip. The second blow took a while.

Snap.

Harris felt the history slipping.

Snap.

He struggled, a little.

Snap.

His father, Sammy, died sometime in '94.

Snap.

Birdy stayed dead.

Snap.

Laura Spinane haunted him.

Snap.

Sarah Hannon.

Snap.

His sister. He never saw her again. The beach was the last vision. The motel was their last —

Snap.

He felt the blood.

The brunette walked around. Her eyes glowed.

She cleaned the crop with her hand.

"I miss you," said Harris.

ACKNOWLEDGEMENTS

Iain would like to thank Carl for his help polishing the cover of this book and for his ongoing support during the writing. Thanks also to J David Osborne whose encouragement and enthusiasm for *Four Days* helped a great deal. His editing didn't hurt either. Finally, my gratitude to Gabriella West who gave this a final going-over.

CONTACT IAIN RYAN

To contact Iain visit IainRyan.com.

He'll write you back. To receive updates, free book excerpts and a collection of 'behind-the-scenes' essays visit iainryan.com/subscribe

83797054R00107

Made in the USA
Lexington, KY
15 March 2018